Amish Vows:

Amish
Rogue

The Final Amish Vows Story

By Rose Doss

Book 6

ISBN: 978-1-955945-33-2

Cover images courtesy of period images and canstockphoto
Cover by Joleene Naylor.

Manufactured/Produced in the United States

PROLOGUE

This book—Amish Rogue—is the final in the series and takes place ten years after Amish Renegade. While each book contains its own, separate romance, these stories are entwined.

This is Sarah Bieler and Mark Fisher's romance. Sarah and Mark were children in the earlier Amish Vows books—Sarah was greatly affected in Amish Renegade by the tough situation in which her father's death left she and her mom. Mark was the surly young boy that Daniel Stoltzfus befriends in Amish Heartbreaker.

The romance between spunky Sarah and unsettled Mark takes place ten years after Amish Renegade, the first in the Amish Vows Series, when Sarah and Mark are grown and establishing themselves. In the process of finding their way, these two interact with all the previous couples in the Amish Vows Series, ten years later…

CHAPTER ONE

Ooph!!

Knocked suddenly off her feet—the volleyball net swimming a little before eyes she blinked open—Sarah felt strong hands reach out to bracket her upper arms.

"Are you all right?"

Blinking again to clear her gaze, she looked up into the handsome face of Mark Fisher.

Bent over her, he looked decidedly cheerful, despite his solicitous question. The fading daylight glinted off his blond head.

"I didn't realize you were so close," he offered, but he looked so cheerful that his words didn't seem like much of an expression of regret.

Feeling a scowl descend onto her face, Sarah retorted, "I'll take that as an apology and point out that I stood no closer than team members usually stand during games."

"*Neh*, really?" His greenish eyes seemed to be laughing at her. "The save was good, though. Did you see it?"

Pulling away from him, Sarah stood and shook sand from her long, full skirt. She responded in a dry voice, "*Neh*. I was too busy falling on my backside to take notice."

Going back to his place to her left, facing the volleyball net, Mark responded with unimpaired satisfaction, "Well, it was *gut*."

"I'm sure it was." She moved back to her spot, trying to discreetly rub the bruised area on her behind. "Remind me to ask not to play next to you again."

From his place, Mark laughed.

Responding to the call for team members to rotate, Sarah shifted.

"Are you okay?" Able Bichsel called from across the net, his face concerned. In the first row of players on the other team, he'd obviously seen Mark bump into her.

"I'm fine." She brushed off the folds of her dusty green skirt. She and Able had gone to school with Mark and she figured Able most likely wasn't surprised at Mark's style of play.

Drat Mark.

The game went on with shrieks from different players as they volleyed the ball back and forth.

Acutely aware of the muscular player to her left, she couldn't help shying away when Mark bounced in her direction. This really annoyed her as she liked the game and was usually the first to go after the ball.

When the players shifted before the next serve, she cast Mark a baleful look as she went to the next row back, positioned now behind Mark Fisher and to his left. *Gott* help her be nice.

Caught up soon in *thwacking* the volleyball across the net when it came her way, Sarah focused on the game, grinning suddenly when the orb came flying back across the net right toward her. With a flash, she saw how she could execute her revenge. Shifting to meet the ball at just the right angle, Sarah hit it toward where Mark stood.

He could have easily hit the ball to send it back across the net—if he'd been looking. If she'd called out a warning that the ball was coming his way. Players often assisted in this way to send the ball over the net when it came from the back row. Remembering his earlier attitude about knocking her over, she didn't give the signal.

Mark wasn't looking for the incoming ball and obviously wasn't expecting it.

She had no intent to send it flying into his head, but that's just where the ball hit, bouncing off the back of his skull with the *thunk* of knuckles on a ripe melon. Clearly, he hadn't suspected this play from a member of his own team. Rubbing his head where the ball had hit, Mark swung around as the team members around him went after the ball.

From across the net, several members of the other team called out for her to join their team.

"Oops," Sarah said with a snigger when she met his scowling gaze. Smirking, she again rotated to allow a new server at the rear.

Ahhh, that had felt *gut.*

Later that evening after the singing, Sarah glanced at her friend, Anna, and then back at the two *Menner* standing across the room. "*Yah*, Mark Fisher is a fine enough *Mann,* I suppose, but he isn't…he doesn't…."

Stopping, she wrinkled her nose at her friend.

Around them, the *Youngies* of their congregation gathered in clustered groups in the plain, serviceable Hochstetler living room, several of the younger *Menner* practicing their corner ball moves at the back.

Every now and then different *Menner* walked past, shooting glances and smiles at Sarah. For the most part, she ignored them, not impressed or interested.

"…but Mark knocked you over in the volleyball game and, besides, he doesn't have a farm or a business to support a *Frau,*" the older girl concluded with an astute summation.

"You can say it like that," Sarah retorted, "but I don't care that much about the game."

She rubbed at her bruised bottom. "I got him back for that, but a *Maedel* needs to think about the future when she chooses a husband. What girl doesn't need to know a *Mann* can support her *Kinder?*"

Stopping, she looked again at the Fisher brothers. "I want to feel safe in my home. To have my eventual children have a home and *Daed* who can care for them."

Glancing at Anna before turning back to look at Mark Fisher and his *Bruder*, she added defensively, "Mark is fun to play a game

4

of volleyball with or to joke with, but he seems aimless and doesn't even care that he has no direction! He may have joined the church, but nothing more. Did I tell you he's taken a job on our farm as a seasonal worker? *Yah*, he's helping my *Daed* plow and plant this spring."

"That should give the two of you plenty of time together," her friend's sideways glance accompanied a small smile.

Readjusting folds of her skirt that still had a smudge on one hip due to Mark Fisher's outrageous playing style, Sarah retorted, "We have more than enough time together for me. Enoch praises him, saying he's so helpful and *schmaert*. Like it takes a miracle to think of plowing the fields in a different order."

"He suggested a different way Enoch could plow?"

Sarah hunched a shoulder. "I guess. It's not like he's saving for a farm, though. I'd be surprised if he's saving, at all."

"He might be and just hasn't mentioned it. *Gott* has told us to be kind to others."

Pulling her mouth into a skeptical expression, Sarah said nothing. The noise in the room rose as the *Frau* of the house and her *Dochders* brought in refreshments now that the singing was over. Several pies and cakes sat at one end of the snowy clean tablecloth while large soft molasses cookies jostled for space at the other end with plates of apple fritters.

How she and Anna had become such friends was a mystery as they were several years apart in age. Sarah's step-mother, Kate, had brought her—a scared, orphaned eight-year-old *Maedel*—along when Kate married her long-time love Enoch. Anna was then Kate's newly-met cousin, who was just fourteen then. The fact that Sarah and Anna were eight years apart in age hadn't mattered though. Just as Sarah considered her younger sister, Elizabeth—only nine now—to be her close friend was an echo of her disregard for age. Elizabeth was a very intelligent girl.

"Enoch has worked his farm for years—ten since he married your mother—and you'd think he'd have seen this better way of plowing the fields," mused Anna in an uncritical voice.

"You'd think," Sarah agreed with a lift of her brows, "but he says he really appreciates Mark's 'advanced ideas', whatever that means. You know Mark Fisher had only agreed to be a temporary worker? I have no idea what he plans to do next, if he even has plans."

"I have no idea, either," Anna murmured.

"You'd think his *Geschwischder* would caution him that he needs some goals. Particularly Grace, his twin sister! But no, it doesn't seem anyone has spoken to Mark about his future."

"Maybe she's not worried about him."

Trying to keep her sour comments from reflecting on her embarrassingly expressive face, Sarah's gaze followed Anna's as they once again gazed across the room. Mark was a well-looking sturdy blond *Mann* of about twenty years, his skin tanned and his eyes more green than blue. That unique eye color was probably the strangest thing about his appearance. No fault could certainly be found in his sturdy frame or with his cheerful, outgoing smile. She sighed almost angrily. How could a *Mann* expect a *Maedel* to get interested in an aimless fellow?

""Bruder! Bruder!" A week later Mark's twin sister, Grace, called out as she ran up the stairs at their home.

"Here." Mark hung his coat on one of the pegs on the wall beside the door in the room he shared with Jakob and young Benjamin.

Grace bounded into the room. "I have such news!"

He grinned at her. They were both blessed with good health and Grace was a very enthusiastic Maedel who looked nothing like him. It had become a joke in their familye.

"Come in and tell me." Of all the people he knew, Mark felt the most comfortable with her. Others might sometimes think him odd or not get his jokes, but Grace was right with him.

His sister collapsed on the bed opposite his.

"John has asked me to marry him!" She fell back on the bed, hugging herself.

Mark laughed. "This has to have been a shock to you, as the two of you have been courting—taking drives and eating with one another's families—for years."

Grace popped up to inform him, "Lots of people take buggy drives together and it means nothing."

"Yah, old Frau Stotle and her sister."

"No. Others, too. Menner and Maedels," she informed him. "Not all marry."

"Very true," he said with a straight face. "I'm shocked that, after spending time with no others and spending all this time together, that you and John have decided to marry."

"Well," she flopped back on the bed. "We could have married others, instead."

"Absolutely," her Bruder responded. "Have you told our parents?"

She sent him a twinkling smile. "Not yet. I will in just a few minutes, but I wanted to tell you first."

"I appreciate that."

Grace giggled.

"You should. Mamm's in the kitchen and I ran right past her to come find you." Her blue eyes laughed at him.

Mark found himself chuckling in response.

Grace bolted into an upright position. "I must ask Mamm for her pickle recipe! I promised John's mother that I'd bring it tonight."

Calling out to her as she streaked past him, Mark grinned. "By all means, tell Mamm and Daed about your marriage! Surprise them! They can't have been expecting this for the last year and a half!"

Grace stuck her head back into his room to make a face at him. This only made him laugh more.

"Tease me all you want, but when are you going to choose a Frau? She demanded in mock severe tones, her hand on her hip.

Waving her words aside, he responded, "Soon enough, Schweschder."

She waggled her fingers at him. "Gut. In the meantime, I know you'll have fun working at Enoch Miller's farm. You can tease Sarah! She's always such fun."

"She is," he agreed, watching his sister disappear from the doorway.

"Shouldn't you sit over there with the young *Menner?*" Sarah asked Mark in bright-eyed challenge at church two weeks later.

Lounging in the chair next to her as he chatted with the Stoltzfus family in the row behind, Mark made a face at her before turning to answer a question Daniel Stoltzfus had asked him. "*Yah*, I'm working as a summer field hand with Enoch. It's been interesting."

He sent a smirking smile Sarah's way. "Most everyone there has been really kind."

"That's *gut*," Daniel commented. "From when you worked with us at the buggy shop when you were a *Youngie*, I know you're a hard worker."

Continuing to look ahead, Sarah grimaced and rolled her eyes. She knew Mark could see the gesture, but probably wouldn't respond.

Out of the corner of her eye, she saw his grin widen as he continued talking with Daniel.

The Stoltzfus family spread along the row behind, sprawling out as only five young *Kinder* could.

The eldest of their children, eight-year-old Jeremiah, sat with solemn correctness two seats from his *Daed*. His seven-year-old sister, Abigail, sat in the seat next to him, her arm around a younger *Bruder* that Sarah recognized as Andrew. Two-year-old Matthew balanced on Daniel Stoltzfus' knee while Lydia, several seats away, cared for their new infant, *Boppli* Rachel.

Glancing at the family, Sarah couldn't help sighing a little. That's what she wanted, what she was determined to have—a lovely cluster of *Kinder*. A kind husband with a solid career.

Daniel was a buggy maker and had taken over Lydia's father shop not too many years back.

It was bizarre that Mark didn't seem to want something as solid for himself.

"*Goedemorgan*, Sarah."

She turned to see Moses Blatter, a *Buwe* from the class just under hers, standing in the walkway, all pink around the ears and smiling awkwardly.

Moses was the son of a small *familye* whose farm was on the west side of town. She'd known him all her life and for years had recognized that he had a crush on her. In the strictest sense, Moses wouldn't have been a bad husband choice for her since he was the only son in the *familye* and their farm would surely go to him.

Sarah smiled perfunctorily. Try as she might, she could never consider him as more than a friend. Still, being rough in her dismissal of him would have seemed mean. "*Goedemorgan*, Moses."

"It's very crowded at services today," Moses offered.

"*Yah*," she agreed, flapping her hand to cool her face. "Meetings almost always are."

"Well," he said, shifting to allow a brisk *Frau* and her flock of *Kinner* to pass. "It was nice seeing you again."

"Very nice." She waved as he moved on, turning back to Mark and the Stoltzfus *familye*.

"You know you're supposed to sit over there!" she whisper-shouted to Mark when his conversation with Daniel ended. Tilting her head toward the area where the young, single *Menner*—including Moses—gathered, she gave an exaggerated sigh.

"No more than you should be sitting with my sister, Grace, and the other *Maedels*," he retorted in a lowered voice, gazing in the direction in which she pointed. "I'm visiting before the service begins, as you are."

"I just know that you don't always follow the rules," she shot back, her voice still only for him to hear, dropping even more quiet when the *Buwe* Jeremiah appeared at Mark's side.

"Not at all." He swiveled back to face forward, as she did, welcoming Jeremiah, Lydia and Daniel's son clambering up on Mark's knee.

"*Hallo*, my *gut* friend!" Daniel's smile broadened as he helped Jeremiah settle in more comfortably.

"You looked lonely up here all by yourself," the boy confided, patting Mark's arm.

"I was," Mark responded seriously, "but not anymore. I'm so glad you came to be with me."

Sarah smiled at the sweet interaction. Even though he seemed aimless, Mark had always been kind to *Kinner*. Her own *Geschwischder* loved him and followed him like baby ducklings after their duck *Mamms*.

Turning back to Sarah, Mark said with a grin. "I'm just not a sheep when it comes to rules, like some. The service hasn't started yet."

"I've seen what you think about rules," she responded, "and I think sheep are wonderful, sweet creatures."

"Maybe they are, but you wouldn't want to court with one."

Turning her head sharply at his words, she said softly, "We aren't courting, either!"

"*Neh!*" His eyes widened in innocent disclaimer as an oblivious Jeremiah played at trotting a carved toy horse along Mark's arm. "I never said we were."

"Besides," she added, as if they hadn't ventured in these deep waters over the top of the small boy's head, "I only came over here to speak to Lydia."

"You aren't speaking to her," Mark pointed out. "She's right there, several seats away."

"I didn't want to interrupt her," Sarah retorted. "I'm waiting till she finishes speaking with *Frau* Bontreger. I have a message for Lydia from my *Mamm*."

"They're finished talking now," he said, nodding toward where Daniel's wife, Lydia, sat holding *Boppli* Rachel.

"*Denki*," Sarah said, tilting her head back to give Mark an insincere smile. "I see that."

She scooted down to a chair several seats away from him to pass on her *Mamm's* message.

Mark watched her go, the zest of their interchange keeping the smile on his face before he looked down to hear something young Jeremiah was saying.

"Are you not coming to take a seat with us?" His *Bruder*, Jesse, said a few minutes later as he passed by the row with his three children—Joel, Levi and little Eve.

The *Haus* was filling now with families and *Mamms* found chairs with their flocks of *Kinder* as everyone began settling down for the sermon.

"*Yah*, I'm coming," Mark responded, smiling at the *Kinder*, all clustered around their *Daed* like little ducklings around a mama duck. "Just visiting with my friend here."

"I see." Jesse laughed, grinning at the *Buwe* on Mark's knee.

The eldest of his *Geschwischder*, Jesse was a widower with young children, and particularly now that he was a widower, Mark tried to help as much as he could. Jesse's *Frau* had died almost a year ago, but the solemn, mourning light still hadn't gone out of his eyes, even when he smiled. Mark knew Grace and their *Eldre*, as well as the other siblings, were helpful whenever possible.

Saying goodbye to Jeremiah a few minutes later, he went to sit with Jesse, scooping up little Eve when she tugged at his pants knee, indicating she wanted to hug him. "Hallo, *Bruder*. Are you and the *Kinder* settling in, now that you've moved back to Mannheim?"

"*Yah*." Jesse rested his arm on the back of young Levi's chair. He grew more serious. "Although it's strange to be here without Hannah."

"I cannot even imagine how that must seem."

His brother's face grew more shadowed and then he looked up to meet Mark's gaze, as if pulling himself up to march on. He sent

11

his *Bruder* a determined smile. "I've been considering what to do now that I'm here. I just…I just don't want to farm now. Hannah and I did that together. Now, I'm thinking of buying the Bontreger's store. I have some money saved and some from selling the farm we left. Didn't you say they had decided to sell now that they're older and want to move closer to the two of their *Dochdars* that live in Steubenville?"

"*Yah*, that is my understanding," Mark responded. He'd always thought Jesse would buy a farm and start over here in Mannheim, but maybe the store might be a better choice. The Bontregers always seemed to make a good living from it.

Later that week, Sarah climbed the stairs from the basement, carrying a bucket of water scooped from the cistern below.

Coming into the kitchen, she plopped the bucket on the floor, reaching out for the mop.

"I still say," she announced to her *Mamm*, "that we should have a Sing here soon."

Kate looked at her with a smile in her eyes. "Because you want us to take note of a special young *Mann*?"

Rolling her eyes, Sarah retorted, "*Neh*, you know I have fun with all my friends, both *Menner* and girls."

"Just asking," her *Mamm* said mildly. "You know this would be your own choice. Both your *Daed* and I know it's a selection you will make yourself."

"Yes." Wringing out the wet mop, Sarah began scrubbing the already-mostly-clean floor. She said in a matter of fact voice, "I've been blessed to live here with the two of you."

Her *Mamm* straightened from the biscuit dough she was rolling out. "What do you mean? Of course, you'd live here with your *familye*."

Shaking her head, Sarah responded, "You know you could have left me with my other *Mamm's* family—the one who died when I was young—or with my father's folk, after he died, too."

"No, I couldn't." Kate went on rolling out the dough. "I fell in love with you when I married Jakob. After he died, you and I were a team."

A tremble of laughter in her words, Sarah said, "And Enoch was only too willing to take me in, as long as that was required to get you. Don't tell me he loved me from the start. You married my other *Daed* straight out of a disagreement with Enoch."

"Enoch is your *Daed*, as much as Elizabeth's or Joshua's. Or any of our other *Kinder*."

"*Yah*, he is and he's been wonderful to me." She paused in mopping, saying reflectively, "But he really loves little Ruthie. I think we all do."

"Ruthie's a *gut* girl," her *Mamm* agreed. "Not that any of us love one in the *familye* more than the other."

"*Neh*. I know it." No matter that they didn't share the same blood, she'd always loved Kate. She knew she was fortunate to have this bond with the woman who was her *Mamm* through marriage. Her friends all loved their mothers, but Kate was beyond price.

"So, no special boy," her *Mamm* teased. "You're getting to the age, though, that *Buwes* are noticing you more. Mark seems extra smiley when you're around."

"I am of an age to start thinking about marrying," Sarah answered with satisfaction, "and I know I want a husband who has more direction than Mark Fisher."

"Why, he seems very nice. Enoch was just telling me the other day how smart Mark is."

"He may be smart," Sarah snapped with more irritation than she had a right, "but he has no direction. Isn't he only working here for the summer?"

"I think it says something," Kate returned, "that he branched out and looked for work other than his father's farm."

"Speaking of outside," Sarah said, wringing out the wet mop again. "I think I'll apply to work at the Bontreger's store. The one they're selling? I think I can do my chores and still work there."

"Oh, that's right." Kate raised her elbow, trying to use it to brush some flour from her cheek. "The Bontregers are selling the store. I think Mark told Enoch his *Bruder* Jesse is looking to buy it, now that they want to move closer to their *familye* in Steubenville."

Mopping a corner to spotlessness, Sarah said, "*Yah*. And you'll think about having a Sing here?"

She added hastily, "Not because I have anyone special, but just that we like having our friends over."

Kate's eyes twinkled. "Of course. *Not* for any one *Buwe*."

"Certainly not!" Sarah plunked the mop again in the bucket.

The next morning, Mark brought the team of four horses plodding to a stop at the end of the row. The creaking of the farm equipment and the crunch of the horses' steps came to a halt as he tugged gently on the reins. Now that the team had stopped, the morning quiet settled all around him, only the faint ripple of birdsong heard in the distance. The dark brown, freshly-plowed dirt field stretched out behind him in gentle, rich ripples. It had, he knew, the farm's richest soil this season.

In peaceful moments like these, he saw *Gott's* handiwork everywhere.

Enoch walked over to meet Mark at the of the row, a broad straw hat shading the *Mann's* strong-jawed face from the late spring sun. So far, this had been a good job with interesting work and a nice *familye*. Having heard the story behind Enoch and Kate's reconnection, Mark respected that no one would ever know Sarah wasn't Enoch's own child. He appeared to treat all his *Kinder* with the same affection.

Mark grinned to himself. He'd been in school a year ahead of Sarah and she was no less spunky now. Fun to tease when he had the time.

"Hallo!" his boss called out before Mark started turning the team to plant the next row of alfalfa. He lifted his voice to say, "I just finished plowing the west field. You can plant that next!"

"Gut." Mark's foot hovered over the pedal that lowered the seeder's prongs. "I should finish this field by lunch and I'll move on to plant that."

"Kate should bring us food about the time you finish seeding here." Enoch adjusted his hat, turning back to work in his matter-of-fact way. Enoch was conservative with his words and Mark could appreciate that, too. As much as he could enjoy a good laugh, he sometimes liked the quiet.

"Okay!" Shifting more comfortably in his seat, Mark lowered his foot as he lifted the reins and spoke to the team, urging it forward to turn and head down the next row. Having grown up on his *Daed's* farm, this job was as familiar as the back of his hand.

Keeping the reins in a steady hold, he started the horses down the next row, their steps as rhythmic and soothing as a rocking chair.

His *Bruders*, Jacob and Benjamin helped their *Daed* on his farm, while Grace and the other girls worked hard with their *Mamm* to keep the house, make food for the family and watch over baby Ezra, if a ten-year-old could be called a *Boppli*. He certainly didn't think so. Even at that age, Ezra was strong and well able to feed the pigs, cows and chickens.

Jacob was to marry his long-time girl that fall and Grace had been courting with the same fellow for two years.

Things were changing all around him, he mused, jolting along the row behind the horses.

Being twins, Grace had told him right away that she thought John Yoder was the one, even though such things were considered private as to avoid any pridefulness. The twins were used to telling each other all their secrets. Mark only hoped that didn't change when Grace was gone out of the *Haus*. It was only with her that he was completely comfortable, truth be told. Of course, all of his *familye* loved him and tolerated his jokes. He couldn't help kidding around sometimes and they seemed to know that about him.

Jogging along as the team crossed the field pulling the seeder, Mark fell into musing about Jesse. The oldest of the *familye's Kinder,* Jesse's recent loss brought them all around him, supporting the *Mann* in his grief. Hannah had been a *gut* wife and a *gut* person. Mark missed her and his concern now was helping his *Bruder.* Apparently, Jesse was abandoning farm life to buy the Bontreger's store.

Best for everyone, it seemed. In the meantime, Mark thought, he enjoyed working with Enoch and Kate's *familye.* Particularly, Sarah.

Later that day, he grinned as he mopped his head before replacing his hat to walk over to where Kate, Sarah and her younger *Schweschder,* Elizabeth, had spread out lunch for the workers in the shade of some trees at the edge of the field.

"*Hallo!*" he called out to where the older sister stood handing out warm rolls to the farm workers. "I'd begun to think you were starving us!"

In reality, lunch was laid out no later than usual. He just liked joking Sarah.

Her eyes flashed as she glanced toward him, pausing to scan his muscular length. "You don't look as though you missed many meals."

"Sarah!" Kate reprimanded her with a smile. "Hush. Don't give Mark a hard time. He's been working all morning. I'm sure he's ready to eat."

"That's right," he retorted. "I'm ready to eat. We workers have to keep up our strength."

She cast him a sour glance. "You seem to be holding on to yours."

Mark grinned. Even when they were *Scholars* sharing a school room, he'd always enjoyed Sarah. She was prettier than most and fun to tease, as well as, easy to rise to his ribbing.

Working on this farm definitely had benefits.

CHAPTER TWO

"I don't need Sarah's help with repairing the cistern!" Mark exclaimed a week later. "Young Joshua can work with me."

"Joshua is only eight-years-old. *Neh*. You'll likely need more help than he can give. It's best, I think, that Sarah do it." Enoch seemed unfazed by his employee's resistance. "He has several more days in school. The cistern needs repair now. It's a two-person job and you'll both probably have to work together in the basement. The top to the cistern needs repair."

Feeling a scowl form on her face, Sarah reminded herself that Mark meant nothing to her personally. He was just another stinky farm helper. Casting him a condescending glance, she looked back at Enoch. "It just needs that one top piece repaired and a new collar. Right? All the rainwater piping is still fine."

She couldn't resist sending Mark a superior glance, proud that she could show off her knowledge of the water system. Wanting to stick her tongue out at him, she resisted, thinking the gesture would be that of a child. She was a grown woman now, well able to help with farm repairs.

"That's right." Enoch sent her a glimmer of a smile. "Just as when we installed it before building the *Haus*."

"I still say I'd be fine without her." Mark's smile was full and irritated her like field brambles. "Seems like you'd be of better use to your *Mamm*."

"You're a worker here," she shot back. "*Daed* assigns us to our jobs."

Opening the basement door for Sarah with a flourish, Mark grinned and gestured for her to take the lead. He wasn't sure she'd be as much help as Enoch thought, but she'd sure be more fun to work with than young *Scholar* Joshua.

A nicely-made *Maedel* of seventeen now with light brown hair beneath her *Kapp* and blue eyes that could laugh or challenge, she was always interesting. He'd noticed her particularly in their small classroom, even though she was a year younger than him. *Gott* bade them to look at the heart, but Sarah's outside wasn't bad, either. It was what he liked to think of as a bonus situation—a good, steady heart packaged in an attractive girl.

He cheerfully followed her down the basement stairs.

The cistern was a large, underground tank that sat beneath the *Haus*, serving as a reservoir for rainwater from various pipes. Built before this structure went up, it was made of cement block and was wide, at least the width of a bedroom. Basically, an underground rain tank, it served to provide the *familye* with water for various needs. It had a cement collar with a covered opening large enough for a bucket to pass through when dipped in to draw water.

In the past, some folk had used clay bricks to form cisterns which, while very effective, could be costly and took time to build. Enoch, being more progressive than some, had built his of concrete block. The cement collar at the top, however, had cracked and needed repair now.

Mark shifted the cistern covering to one side. Only an echo—and a tiny splash when a pebble fell in—indicated the vast expanse of water beneath them.

With the cistern cover put aside to give access to the collar surrounding the whole, he glanced over to see how his helper liked the dark, gloomy basement, Mark saw that Sarah was off to the side, rearranging jars of stored food stuff on a shelf. She didn't seem at all fazed by her surroundings.

"*Mamm* and I put these pickles and beets up from our garden last year. I've been meaning to come down and organize the shelves," Sarah commented, clearly not afraid of the spider-filled darkness.

The great cistern beneath them made a hollow, other-worldly sound that, when the cap was removed, echoed through the basement.

Mark had left the door at the top of the basement stairs open for light and there were several high, grimy windows along a far wall, contributing a pale light to the basement gloominess.

"Are you sure no creepy crawlies will come get you?" he asked with laughter in his voice.

Sarah rolled her eyes at him. "If they do, I'll make sure they get you first."

Laughing at her practical response, he looked around for a fat, juicy spider to fling at her. She was fun to tease and he wanted to see if she was as matter-of-fact as she sounded. Sadly, all the spiders seemed to be hiding in the darkness,

Sarah came away from the shelf, standing next to him to examine the cistern collar.

When he inhaled, he drew in her clean scent and a floral smell that seemed at odds with the muted green of her dress.

She bent down, her black *Kapp* close to the cistern collar. "I can see that it's cracked. *Daed* was right to send us to do a repair."

"We will need a bag of cement," he commented. "I suppose that will be too heavy for you to bring down?"

Again, she rolled her eyes at him. "We will also need another bucket for mixing it. I believe the water bucket is already next to the cistern."

She went trotting up the stairs to get the extra bucket and the cement.

"I'll be right back," Sarah said as she ascended, adding in a sassy voice, "Maybe, in the meantime, you can clean away the broken collar chunk."

"*Yah*," he laughed, calling up after her. "I'll do that."

Together, they worked in the dim basement, Mark pouring the powdery cement into the water in the bucket while she looked around for a stick to stir it.

"You'd probably rather be baking in the kitchen or hanging laundry out to dry."

Shaking her head, she said, "You've obviously have never hung laundry on the line."

Mark chuckled. "You could be quilting with your *Mamm* and your *Schweschder*, Elizabeth. She knows how to quilt? Young Elizabeth?"

"Of course, Lizzie is already nine. She does many things."

"I bet you quilt better than her and bake better, too."

"I've been doing these many years longer. Practice always makes better." Sarah sounded exasperated.

He didn't know why, but her reaction pleased him. Mark liked getting a rise out of her.

"Have you repaired cisterns before?" She looked up at him, her brows lifted. "Your *Daed* must have one on his farm."

"*Yah*. I think Jesse and Jakob helped him when this needed repair years ago."

She stared at him a moment. "You're not working on his farm?"

"*Neh*. I did before, but Jakob handles most of the farm chores now himself. *Daed* still works with him some. Jesse moved away with his *Frau* years back. Now that she's no longer with us, Jesse and his three young *Kinder* have moved back. He's buying the Bontreger's store and will work there."

He glanced over at her where she knelt next to him beside the cistern collar, her light brown hair visible at her neck, just below her *Kapp*. Her neck rose above the dress and he looked back at the cement, taking a deep breath to squelch the urge to draw her into his arms and bury his face there.

That would startle her. Mark smiled at the directions of his thoughts.

Looking down again at the dark water in the cistern below, she asked, "And you work here with my *Daed* on his farm? Not with Jakob or with Jesse at the store?"

"For this part of the summer, I work here with Enoch. Jacob has the farm running very smoothly." Mark again smoothed the trowel over the wet cement, "and Jesse hasn't yet completely taken over the store. I've been thinking that when Enoch no longer needs me here in a few weeks, I might like to work with Gideon Lapp at his forge. He's taking on some help as there will be heavy work coming up at the beginning of the summer."

"So, even though you were raised on a farm and work here with Enoch, you don't feel you must keep working the land?"

"*Neh*," he responded cheerfully, "I like trying new things."

"You don't feel you should settle down and build something of your own? Like take a section of your *Daed's* farm?"

"Jacob wouldn't like that," he responded unresentfully. "Benjamin and young Ezra have already expressed interest in getting farmlands—and Ezra's just a *Youngie. Neh.* I'm still looking around."

"I would think," she said, dusting off her hands, "that having joined the church already after your *rumspringa*, you'd be ready to settle down. Get a *Frau* and start a *familye* of your own."

Mark said, "There's time for all that. No need for haste."

Looking at him for a moment with a lack of expression that was unusual for her, Sarah turned away, walking over to look at the shelves there. Continuing to trowel the cement carefully, he glanced at her. She was such a spitfire, he'd have expected her to give her opinion about where he should work.

Reaching over to the water bucket—knowing that throwing cement around wasn't a *gut* idea—he dipped his fingers in and flicked them at her.

Having been examining the shelves, as if mentally rearranging them, her head was turned away.

When the water droplets showered over her, she turned back to him, saying with severity, "Attend to the matter at hand, you *dumm hund!*"

"I don't know what you're talking about," he claimed with false innocence.

She made a face at him, shaking her head.

"You must be imagining things," Mark insisted, hiding his amusement.

Looking down at the water droplets darkening her dress, she said in a tart voice, "I'm going to be 'imagining' myself dumping the entire bucket of water over you, if you do that again."

Giving a shout of laughter that echoed around the gloomy basement, he protested, "What do you mean? I'm stirring the concrete."

"And I suppose," Sarah responded in a withering accent, "these wet drops on my dress are because it's raining down here? I remember what a jokester you've always been. Don't try to fool me."

"You do have wet spots on you!" he said in an amazed voice, as if he'd just noticed.

She made a disgusted sound in her throat. "Let's just get the cistern collar repaired and be done with it."

"I don't know," he continued to stir the cement, "whatever work I do next will likely be in the warm sun. It's cool down here and very pleasant, if you don't mind the bugs in the corners and the sassy company."

"I'm not the one throwing water," she reminded him kindly.

He chuckled.

Together they knelt beside the cistern collar, a bucket of cement between them, and Mark used a trowel to reach into the bucket she held steady. He mounded the wet cement around the cistern opening, lodging a trowel-load into the broken section.

"You probably wish the *Buwe* with whom you're visiting was here doing this work," he commented with mock seriousness.

"I'm visiting with lots of *Menner*," she replied, his teasing earning a head-shaking from her to go along with her smile. "Besides, you preferred to work with my little *Bruder*. I heard you tell my *Daed*. So, don't act like being here with me was your first preference, *Denki* very much."

"I just wasn't wanting an unwilling helper," he protested. "I thought you'd rather be baking or hanging out laundry."

"I'm going to remember this," she promised, "and when we do laundry next week, I'll ask *Daed* to set you to help, since you think laundry is so much fun."

Five days later, Sarah knelt next to the repaired cistern collar, drawing up the rope that held a bucket of rainwater. Morning light streamed through the low basement windows, casting oblong blocks of light on the basement floor.

"And you worked down here with Mark all that morning?" Anna said.

"*Yah.*"

Anna smiled at her, a twinkle in the other girl's eyes. "He is a nice-looking *Buwe*. Fun, too."

"And he knows it! Both of those things, no doubt." Sarah stood, holding the water bucket carefully to pour it out into the one she'd brought down from the kitchen. "He's very full of himself. *Gott* has said we are not to be proud...and Mark doesn't have any drive, that I can see."

"Only *Gott* knows the heart," Anna said softly. "You know that."

"This is true." Sarah emptied the cistern bucket into the larger one, "but we here, on this Earth are to use the *schmaerts Gott* gave us to make our decisions. I cannot doubt that Mark will find a *Maedel*. I just hope he finds work he likes and makes enough to support a *familye*."

Her friend sat on the lowest step of the basement stairs.

Shaking her head, Anna said, "At least, for all his faults, Mark seems like an honest *Mann*. Some are not."

"Oh! I'm sorry, Anna." Sarah reached out a contrite hand, distressed that she'd upset the other girl. "I never meant to remind you. That Hiram you married seemed like a nice *Mann*, too. You are not to blame yourself! His leaving the church and running off was his sin."

In the last few months, Anna had regained a little of her brightness, her smiles coming easier. Sarah hated having brought back all the anguish her friend had faced through no fault of her own.

Her gaze lowered, Anna said in a strained voice, "I am not so sure. It's easy to say all was his fault, but I wonder…if I'd been a better wife, would he have gone?"

"You were a very *gut* wife," Sarah insisted staunchly. If anyone deserved loyalty in a friend or a husband, it was her. "You were! Hiram couldn't have found a better *Frau*. You've had terrible luck, through no doing of your own. I'm just glad that you're a widow now and free to find another *Mann*."

With a sad smile, Anna responded, "*Neh*. I don't want that. Besides, Hiram's leaving has left a stain on me. Even if he did die in a bar brawl, I'm not likely to be appealing to another *Mann*. People prefer to stay away from trouble."

"My friend," Sarah came away from the cistern, having lowered the metal covering, "you aren't stained. *Gott* knows your heart, as well. He has His hand over you and will make this all work out."

Looking down again, Anna said, "I can only keep praying for sustenance and comfort; that and ask for forgiveness."

"You know you have that," Sarah responded swiftly, "not that Hiram's actions were your choice, but *Gott* loves us and forgives us, if we seek Him."

Several days later, Sarah knelt before a dusty set of shelves in what had been Bontreger's store, scrubbing away with a damp rag.

"Excellent work," said her boss, Jesse Fisher, as he passed by.

Like his *Bruder*, Mark, Jesse had blond hair and green eyes, only he was several years older. His hair was a little darker blond and he seemed preoccupied all the time, which Sarah could understand. Not only was he taking over a business he'd never before run, but he was a widowed *Daed* to three adventurous *Kinder*.

Sarah already liked the *familye*.

"The shelves needed a *gut* cleaning," she responded cheerfully as the tinkling bell at store door could be heard.

Jesse hurried to the front and she used the bucket of water beside her to clean the rag before passing it one more time over the shelf. Restocking the items she'd set on the floor beside her, she leaned back to get a better look at the shelf she'd just arranged. Having set the containers and boxes in neatly regimented rows, Sarah shifted a jar, placing the label facing forward.

Orderliness and organizing were restful to her, so what might be drudgery to others wasn't unpleasant to her. She also enjoyed meeting with and serving her neighbors, so working the front register also seemed like nice work, too.

As the store was usually busy with shoppers, she didn't stop her work for the usual murmur that could be heard from the register at the front of the store.

"She's back there, cleaning shelves," she heard her boss say then.

"*Hallo!*" Anna smiled as she came around the row of shelves. "You seem busy."

"*Hallo*, Friend." Sarah smiled back. "I've been back here most of the day, cleaning and reorganizing the things on these shelves. They were terribly dusty!"

Anna sat down on a short stool that was nearby. "So, enjoying yourself, I'd say."

Sarah laughed. "*Yah*. Very much. And do you know I'm making money doing what I'd do at home?"

"That's how it works," Anna responded with a chuckle. "That was your boss? The *Mann* at the register? He seems nice."

"He is. Jesse Fisher. He's a widow and he has the cutest three little *Kinder*." Sarah grew somber. "Their *Mamm* died sometime last year. That's why Jesse decided to move closer to home."

"Oh, that's right. He's Mark Fisher's older *Bruder*. I remember him from school. He's always seemed nice."

"*Yah*." She wrung her rag again after dipping it in the bucket. "Mark comes by sometimes to play with the two little *Buwe's* and their younger sister."

"That's kind of him."

"It is. He and Jesse seem close." Stretching to reach a far shelf corner, she ducked inside the shelves.

Just then the thunder of running feet could be heard as two young *Scholars* ran by, both boys looking like their *Onkle* Mark and their *Daed*. Both wore dark suits like Jesse, although theirs were dusty and seemed short on their growing legs.

"Slow down!" Sarah called out. "You don't want to run down old *Frau* Swartz who sometimes shops here."

"Yes, Sarah," the eldest, Joel, called as he reached out to snag his younger brother.

"Their little *Schweschder*, Eve, is around here somewhere." Sarah wrung the rag out in the bucket again, moving up to clean the next shelf. "They're here, driving their *Daed* distracted, since school's out for the summer."

As if to underline what she said, Jesse could be heard admonishing the boys not to run wildly through the store and to mind their little sister.

"Eve is only four, I think," Sarah said, wiping the higher shelf. "She's the cutest thing with blonde curls sticking out from under her *Kapp*."

Just then Jesse rounded the corner, holding his chastened sons at the back of their necks. "Have you seen Eve? Joel and Levi said she was out back earlier, playing in the dirt, but I don't find her there now."

Chuckling at the profoundly innocent expressions on the boys' faces, Sarah commented, "I think they need a keeper, as you're very busy here. Oh, I'm sorry! This is my friend, Anna Hershberger."

"*Hallo*," Anna said in a shy voice, giving Jesse an embarrassed smile.

"How are you *Buwes* today?" she asked the two *Scholars*, seeming more natural. "I would think you'd rather be outside, running in the fields than dodging through the store."

"*Hallo, Frau* Hershberger," their father responded for them when they said nothing beyond muttering, "Yes, Ma'am. They would do better running in fields."

He shook his sons' necks. "I must be here, though."

Without even thinking, Sarah blurted out, "Anna is a widow, like you."

Her friend's cheeks turned pink at her words and Sarah blundered on, knowing she shouldn't have said anything, but not sure how to change the subject.

"She lives with her *Mamm* in a little *Haus* not far from here."

"You know," Anna commented to the boys as if Sarah hadn't spoken. "I have a fun game that might keep you occupied for a while. Shall I teach you?"

"Can we, *Daed*?" Levi craned the neck his *Daed* still held to look up at Jesse.

"I'm sure *Frau* Hershberger is too busy right now." He glanced over at Anna. "Did you not have shopping to do?"

Still pink, she shook her head. "I came in to see Sarah. I can teach them the game."

She looked at the two boys, "We can find your little sister and see if she'd like to learn, too."

Joel stepped away from his father's hand. "That would be great."

"Fine, then," Jesse said, releasing Levi, "but you must thank *Frau* Hershberger."

The boys raced ahead, skipping toward the store's front door.

Anna glanced over to Jesse. "Please don't keep calling me *Frau*. Just Anna will do."

"Of course," he replied a little awkwardly.

With a wave of her hand to Sarah, she scurried out after Joel and Levi.

"Don't mind her," Sarah said when her friend disappeared around the shelves. "Anna's a widow herself. Well, she is now."

Her boss turned to look at her with lifted brows. "Now?"

Cursing her slip of the tongue, she could have cried with relief when Mark Fisher came into the store aisle.

"*Hallo!*" he called out. "Are the *Kinder* ready for a playmate? I'm through at the forge today, since Gideon doesn't have any more work for me."

Her embarrassment at nearly gossiping about her best friend motivated Sarah to say sarcastically, "Really? It's amazing how little work you manage to do."

Not noticeably distressed by this remark, he responded. "I do make it look that way. I'm just very, very fast in getting work finished. Are the *Kinder* around?"

As Mark had directed this last question to Jesse, his *Bruder* replied, "Sarah's friend, Anna Hershberger went out to play with them."

"That was kind of her."

"Anna is kind," Sarah said, eager to present her friend in the best light. "You know, she'd be a *gut* one to help you with the children! *Kinder* always like her as she's very gentle and fun."

"I bet having the *Kinder* under foot is slowing you down in getting to know this place," Mark joked to Jesse.

His brother's beard twitched with his small smile, but Jesse just said, "I like them being around."

"Of course, you do," Mark countered, "but watching them does give you another concern."

"Anna could watch them for you, could bring them here to see you for visits," Sarah added, "and them take them back to your *Haus* when they need distraction and you need to work."

A considering look settled onto Jesse's face. "That...that might be for the best and Anna has no other work? I wouldn't want to steal her from her *familye*."

"As long as she's earning a wage and having a *gut* time with your *Kinder*, she and her *Mamm* will be happy."

"Which would be good for you, as well, what with you getting the store in order," Mark added. Although he was only in the store to help Jesse, he turned away to answer a customer's question.

"*Hallo*, Sarah," interrupted Timothy Musselman, who'd walked down the store aisle behind Hannah Oberli and her mother. He was a boy of Sarah's age with unruly brown hair and a cheerful smile, who had finished school at the same year as she and Mark. Sarah had played with both Timothy and Hannah Oberli, who was even now shooting dagger darts out of her blue eyes to where Timothy and Sarah talked.

"I didn't know you were working here." He leaned with apparent unconcern on the shelf she'd been cleaning.

"I am working here now. I just started," Sarah confided. She glanced at his companions, stopped just down the aisle to look with great deliberation at the shelves.

Lowering her voice, she said laughingly, "And I didn't know you and Hannah Oberli were seeing one another. She doesn't seem very happy with you."

Ignoring her observation, Timothy sent Hannah what appeared to be a reassuring smile. "Oh, we've known each other forever. You know, as you and I have. I was passing in the lane outside when they asked me in while they shopped for a few things."

"Of course," Sarah replied, keeping to herself her observation that Hannah's interest in Timothy seemed more than casual. He was a very nice *Buwe* who worked the large *familye* farm with his *Daed* and two *Bruders* and would, no doubt, set up one of his own soon. Some families were well able to set up several sons on farms of their own and the Musselman's were among these.

"We're going on to the next row," Hannah called out to Timothy, her expression almost painfully pleasant. "Oh, *hallo*, Sarah. I didn't notice you there."

Looking down as she wrung out her wet rag in her bucket, Sarah repressed her quiver of a smile. Afterall, she understood the importance of a *Maedel* finding a *gut* husband. "*Hallo*, Hannah."

"Well, I'll see you around," Timothy said, sauntering down the aisle toward Hannah.

"Goodbye!" Sarah couldn't help smiling as she started again wiping the shelf.

Free now to pick up her interrupted conversation with her boss—standing several feet away and attending to a display of cans while she'd spoke to her friends—she said, "I'm sure Anna would be very *gut* at watching your *Kinder*. She's well-liked by children."

Mark seemed to have disappeared while she spoke to Timothy and Hannah and that was probably for the best. He knew them as well as she did, but she didn't want to hear any teasing remarks from him about Timothy as an option or discuss with him how she was faring in choosing a husband from their friends.

To her relief, he only reappeared now after the others had moved on.

"*Yah*," Jesse responded." I think having Anna look after the kids would give them a break from being at the store. They'd like that. We're still getting settled in here.

He turned his head to say to his brother, "I'm glad I have a good worker here in Sarah. She's cleaning these dusty shelves, as you can see. The Bontreger's must have had their hands full for some time. These shelves need a good cleaning."

"Sarah is a *gut* worker," Mark agreed, grinning at her. "I'm surprised they could spare her at the farm. You should see her repair a cistern."

"You make too much of that," she admonished with a shake of her head.

"And," Mark laughingly went on, "she can quilt, cook, make candles, can jams and jellies, mind the other *Kinder* and sew. All at the same time."

Sarah rolled her eyes, laughing as she agreed, "*Yah*. All at the same time."

Jesse frowned in confusion. "I thought you worked on a big farm. Others work there, too."

"*Yah*, Jesse. You know your *Bruder*. Always teasing," she said, laughing in spite of herself. It was annoying that this *Mann*, who frustrated her, could also joke her into mirth..

CHAPTER THREE

Later that week, the 'smithy door closed behind resolute, little, nine-year-old Esther Lapp as Mark watched Gideon Lapp shift several horseshoes in the forge. The intensity from the fire tightening the skin of his face, Mark leaned in, observing his boss' skill.

This was a *gut familye* to be around. He'd been lucky in these last two jobs. Some folk weren't happy at home and it showed. Working with Gideon's happy bunch was generally as enjoyable as Enoch and Enoch's *familye*. Sarah was particularly fun!

Gott had directed him to some really *gut* jobs.

"And you started learning this when you were just a *Youngie!*" he said to Gideon. "It must be like breathing now, if you could breathe in this heat."

Gideon just laughed. "*Yah.* It can get a little warm, but I don't mind. Ben Hershberger was a very *gut Mann.* I must have been ten or twelve when I started moving things around in the shop for him. Like you're doing now."

Shaking his head, Mark commented. "Just older than your young *Dochder?* You must have been a strong ten-year-old. Weren't you working with your own *Daed* then?"

Pulling the tongs out of the fire, Gideon leaned them against the big forge.

"I was strong enough, although I felt like a string bean then. All arms and legs and knobby knees. I was here a lot. My *Daed* worked a small, rented farm. We weren't ever hungry, but our family was large and when Ben noticed me hanging around here to play with Hagar and Peter, my friends, Ben offered me work."

"You seem to have taken to it. Do you think your own *Kinder* will follow in your footsteps?"

"Hard to say. James is just seven. Of course, if *Maedels* became blacksmiths, Esther might have run my shop." Gideon laughed. "We named her right. She's like her *Grossmammi* Esther was, but bossier."

"*Yah*," Mark laughed. "She's quite a steady, dependable girl."

Pretty, too—in her direct, *Scholar* way—which never hurt.

"Of course, we hope to have more *Kinner*, so maybe a son will work here." Gideon didn't seem to feel strongly about it one way or the other. "I'll find someone to take the shop on when I'm old and gray."

Mark observed, picking up a broom to sweep a corner of the shop. "What did you use this area for? I can't see you sitting in the rocking chair."

His employer was easy to talk with, but Mark couldn't see him lounging around much.

"*Neh*," Gideon responded with a smile, looking at a small area that was sectioned off at the back of the shop.

As befit his profession, he was a tall *Mann* with bulging arm muscles. "Years ago—before we married—Hagar rocked Eli there."

Stopping to stare at his employer, Mark said, "Eli? Your *Bruder's Kleinzoon*? Why he's a big, strapping *Buwe* now, of, at least nine or ten. I could see him as a blacksmith, but he's not even Hagar's *Kinder*. Why would she rock him here? Didn't his *Mamm* want to keep him home?"

"As you know, Leah is my *Nibling*," Gideon said, not answering the question directly. "For a time, Eli liked napping here. He was a *Boppli* who didn't mind noise."

Knowing better than to ask further, prying questions, Mark just commented, "Different *Bopplin* like different things."

"*Yah*," Gideon responded. "Have you finished moving those pieces of metal? I'm about to get busy as the farming season winds down. I thought I might as well clear the shop now."

"This is certainly different than the work I did before," Mark offered in a jaunty tone. He liked trying new things and this was certainly new.

Gideon's big hammer came down with a crash before he looked over. "I'm sure. You worked at Enoch and Kate's place?"

"I did, but you'd think Sarah ran the place, as much as she knows about it. She even worked with me to repair the cistern collar. Enoch said she'd be of more help than her young *Bruder* and he was right." Mark grinned at Gideon over his shoulder, his smile bubbling up as he thought about spunky, sassy Sarah. He liked her fiery responsivity. "She's more fun to work with, too."

Shifting the horseshoe on his anvil, the big *Mann* said, "Sarah's the oldest *Maedel* in that *familye*, isn't she?"

"*Yah*, she's only a year younger than me. We were in the school together."

"The kind of *Maedel* that makes you think about settling down?" Gideon asked with a twinkling smile.

"It'll be a while before I settle down," Mark responded, leaning the broom in a corner, pausing to stretch his arms over his head. "I like looking around. Trying new things."

"Take my advice, young *Mann*. Don't wait too long to settle down in one spot with one *Maedel*. I almost lost my heart when I did that. Hagar nearly married another. I finally realized what I wanted." He beamed. "Hagar and I have three *Kinder* in our *familye* and, like I said, hope to have more."

"I'll settle down with one girl eventually. I have to find the right place for me, though," Mark replied, starting to clear another corner of the blacksmith shop. "I might want to become a blacksmith, like you. Maybe I'll end up working in a forge."

"How's working in the blacksmith job?" Grace asked, coming to sit next to her brother on the porch swing later that day, an apple in her hand.

"Hot," Mark responded wryly.

"I can imagine," she nodded. "That forge must really warm up the place."

"To put it mildly," Mark said, smile as he lifted his eyebrows at her.

"What have you and *Mamm* and the other girls been up to?"

"Claudia and Amity were sent to get some items from Bontreger's—oh, I mean Jesse's—store. *Mamm* and I," she said, lowering her voice, "planted some more celery in the garden."

Mark felt his eyebrow lift. "What? Didn't you plant some before? And why are you whispering?"

"You know marriages aren't spoken of! We wouldn't want to appear proud or to seem to be bragging about my getting married."

"*Neh.*" He squinted at her, not sure how to connect all the dots.

"Surely," she said in a severe tone, you know we must have a wedding dinner and that celery will be a part of this. No one needs to know *Mamm* and I planted more celery!"

"*Neh,*" he said, laughing at her intensity. "How are the preparations going? Have you started sewing your dress?"

"Yes, it's the loveliest blue. Like the sky."

Mark nodded. "*Gut.*"

"Working with Gideon must be nice," she commented, taking a bite of her apple.

"It is," he agreed. "Gideon's a very nice fellow. Patient with those who are learning."

"You'll learn fast," she said confidently. "You wouldn't allow less of yourself."

"I appreciate your belief in me." Mark reached over to pat her knee through her muted blue dress. "You're a *gut* twin."

"*Yah,* I am," she agreed, turning to toss her apple core into a nearby bush. "I know that if you don't learn this fast, you'll be a bear to live with."

He broke out laughing, but wasn't able to disagree with her. "Are you already working with hot metal from the forge? Doesn't he need to go over safety practices with you?"

"I'm working with the horseshoes and the forge. As to safety practices, you just need to avoid touching hot stuff."

Grace laughed, "I can see that!"

"Do not gulp your food, James," Hagar admonished fondly the next day.

Taking marginally smaller bites at about the same speed, her son managed to say through a mouthful, "Sammy and Joel will be here soon, *Mamm*."

She brushed a hand over his sandy head. "Lots of people will be here soon. That's no reason to act like you've never eaten before."

"You heard your *Mamm*," Gideon interjected, taking a seat near his son at the table. "You've seen us readying the *Haus*. You know it'll be filled up for the service soon."

"Yes, *Daed*." James slowed another smidgeon.

Beside him, his twin ate almost as quickly.

"Who wants to help me finish setting out the chairs?" Mark asked. "We'll make a race of it to see who finishes first."

"I do!" mumbled Anna, James' twin sister.

Truthfully, James reminded Mark more of his own twin *Schweschder*, Grace, and Anna seemed more like Mark, but both were lively and fun.

"Okay, but you must finish your breakfast—not by gulping the food your *Mamm* has made you," he hastened to add. "When you are finished—slowly—we can have our race."

"*Yah*." Anna took unbelievably slow spoonful, chewing with exaggeration.

"I can eat slower than you," James announced, himself shifting into an imitation of a decrepit turtle.

Mark watched the *familye*, affectionately remembering his own youth. He sent a silent prayer of thanks to *Gott*. His *Eldre* had been very *gut* parents to all their *Kinder*, even handling the *verhaddelt* period he'd gone through. His *Grossdaddi* had helped a lot, of course, when he was a mixed-up kid, directing him toward Daniel Stoltzfus. In his own, admittedly careless way, Mark hoped he'd be as helpful to those around him as Daniel had been to him.

Mark smiled, remembering that Apple, the now-aged horse Daniel had helped him gentle when Mark was in this rough time, was supposed to come into Gideon's forge to get shoes later that week.

The kitchen door opened just then, slamming shut behind Gideon with his eldest *Dochder* following behind. "Chores finished! That breakfast smells *gut*, doesn't it, Esther?"

"Very," said the slender child, slipping into a chair next to James.

"I'm so glad you could come early this morning," Hagar said, pausing to put a warm slice of frosting-laden apple-cinnamon bread on Mark's plate. "It's good to have help getting ready for the service."

"Particularly with only these really-slow *Kinder* to help," Mark said, suppressing a smile.

"You told us to eat slowly!" Anna sputtered.

"*Yah*, but you two are really slow," he teased. He preferred making sly remarks to Sarah Beiler, as she was both pretty and sparky, but these two would do.

Gideon went to where his *Frau* stood at the stove, leaning in for a smacking kiss before she shooed him back to sit at the table and have his breakfast.

"So," the big *Mann* said cheerfully, taking a seat next to Mark. "What do you think of blacksmithing? Might this be your work in life?"

"Could be," Mark responded, just as cheerfully. "I'm still looking around. There's time yet."

"Is your *Bruder*, Jesse, settling in? I was in the store just yesterday to pick up a few things. It looks like he's cleaning and reorganizing all the shelves. Sarah's a *gut* help, I'm sure."

"She is," Mark nodded between bites, "and they're getting a lot done, particularly now that Jesse has Sarah's friend watching the *Bopplin*."

"*Yah*," Gideon reached to snag a slice of apple bread, "Anna Hershberger is helping out, is she not?"

Hagar laughed. "She is, but I don't think Joel and Levi consider themselves *Bopplin*."

"Probably not." Mark grinned. "I think I should drop in on Jesse and Sarah—"

"Particularly Sarah," Gideon contributed before taking a mouthful of bread.

Laughing a little ruefully, Mark agreed. "Particularly. Just to make sure she's keeping everyone in line."

A week later, Jesse left his ledger books at his desk, adjusting his hat as he left to open the store. Despite the heat of the day growing, the morning air still felt fresh on his face.

His three *Kinder* were outside, helping Anna Hershberger collect eggs from the hen house.

Even though he didn't farm now—renting his fields to others in the church—and his newish house had no barn to loom over it, they did have a hen house with many *Hinkel* to provide fresh eggs. A cantankerous goat also roamed the property, providing milk for the *Kinder*.

Jesse descended the *Haus* porch, heading back to the shed that provided shelter for his buggy and horse, Willow.

Thankfully, Anna was good with both caring for the hens and milking the goat. She didn't mind tending to Willow, when he was too busy and the children liked her a lot. Even little Eve seemed to be coming out of her grief at losing her *Maam*.

Anna was a Godsend and he'd ever be grateful that Sarah had introduced them.

Beside his buggy a few moments later, he paused before getting into the seat behind the horse. Across the yard, Joel, Levi and little Eve, in her tiny black *Kapp*, were playing a game of tag with Anna behind the *Haus*.

He smiled, hearing their shrieks of glee as they chased after Anna. She seemed really aware of the difference in their sizes—of her being grown and them only small—not racing away from them, as she could. Dodging with surprising agility around a bush in the back yard, she ran around one pole at the end of the clothesline and then around the sturdy iron water pump. Fair-haired Levi just behind her, his hat having tumbled off somewhere.

"You can't get me!" she yelped out. "Don't catch me! Please, don't catch me."

Jesse stood unmoving, stopped in his work-a-day progress by the rippling sound of the *Kinders'* laughter. He hadn't heard his three being so joyful in…in a long, long time.

"I caught you, Anna!" Eve called out, her arms thrown around Anna's skirts as the boys caught her by the arms.

Moisture prickled behind his eyes and Jesse cleared his throat, sending up a prayer of thanks to *Gott* for sending Anna into his children's lives.

She stopped, laughing breathlessly, ringed all around by the three smaller bodies. Cradling Eve close in one arm, she patted Levi's bare head at the same time. "We should go in now, you three, and have some animal crackers or beet chips."

Jesse drew a deep, ragged breath, knowing his poor Hannah would weep with relief to see her children in such *gut* care.

"Can I have pretzels?" Joel asked in a carrying voice as they all walked toward the *Haus* where Jesse stood by the buggy.

"Of course, you can." Anna smiled at the elder boy. "As long as you wash the dust off your hands first."

The four of them walked up to where Jesse stood, Anna looking up with a breath-takingly happy expression on her face.

For a moment, his heart seemed to have stopped. He'd not realized before how lovely she was.

"Are you headed to the store?"

She smiled at him, not apparently noticing his captivated state.

Jerking to consciousness, Jesse managed to say, "*Yah*. Just now."

"Have a *gut* day," Anna called, the clump of her and his children sweeping past him.

With their disappearance into the kitchen, he climbed into his buggy, scrubbing a hand over his face before starting the horse off down the driveway.

It was really nothing, Jesse tried convincing himself. *Kinder* played. Anna's job was to play with them.

Looking blindly over the horse's back, he wondered why the moment had felt so much like…something

Laughing softly, Anna told Levi later that afternoon, "Turn around. I will brush the garden dirt off your backside."

His arms were laden with a pile of the weeds that she and the boys had uprooted from the garden plot behind their *Haus*.

The small boy turned, standing with his armful of weeds while she dusted the clumps of damp soil off him.

"There. You can dump those in the composting area."

"*Denki*." He trotted down the row and out the gate in the fenced garden.

Just on the other side of the fencing, Eve was bent as she studied something in the grass.

"Don't eat it, Evie! Whatever it is," Anna called out humorously.

The girl lifted her gaze to Anna, calling out in her solemn, expressionless voice, "I found some lady beetles."

"She means lady bugs," Joel said, pulling weeds near the fence line at the end of the garden. "My *Mamm* called them that. Lady beetles."

"Don't hurt them, Eve," Anna called out. "They're good for the garden."

The young girl went back to studying the grass.

"It must be difficult," Anna said softly to Joel after a few minutes of silence, "not having your *Mamm* with you."

He lifted his sandy head, looking at her with a somber expression like his sister's.

Not wanting to pressure the *Buwe* into a discussion he didn't want to have, she went back to clearing the dirt around her.

"It is," Joel responded after a pause. "She was…. *Mamm* loved us very much."

Anna looked up at him. "This can seem to make the loss worse. At least, that's how it seemed with my *Daed*."

Joel said nothing, just gazing at her.

"I was older than you when my *Daed* got sick and died," she went on, still wrestling a stubborn root out of the dirt. "It had been the three of us—*Daed*, *Mamm* and me—all my life. A smaller *familye* than those around us, but happy until then."

"That is a small *familye*," the boy said slowly. "Ours was bigger when my *Mamm* was alive."

She glanced at him, hearing a grieving boy behind his matter-of-fact words.

"It must be very hard. Not having a *Mamm*," Anna said in her gentle tone. "I love my *Mamm* very much."

Joel bent his head over the patch of dirt. He made no response.

She went on. "Your *Daed* must feel so blessed to have you and your *Geschwischder* to comfort him.

Swallowing, the boy said stoutly, "*Yah*. He is a *gut Daed*."

"He is a very *gut Daed*," Anna agreed. "He's working hard to keep you and your *Geschwischder* safe and cared for. And we're all with friends. Everyone here—your *Grossdaddi* and *Grossmammi*. Your *Daed's* brothers and sisters."

Joel drew a deep breath. "*Yah*, them and all our friends."

Glancing up at Hagar and Gideon's *Haus* a week later as Mark led a horse into Gideon's forge to be shod, he saw Sarah coming away from visiting Hagar.

He grinned. Mark hadn't seen pretty Sarah Bieler in days, now that he didn't work on Enoch's farm.

Sniggering in private glee, he hid himself, knowing the path she took would lead her around the corner of the blacksmithing shed. This would be good, as she was always such fun to tease.

Just as she rounded the corner of the 'smithy, he jumped forward, the hand not holding the horse's reins up, he yelled, "Boo!"

Startled Sarah jumped back at his shout.

"Mark!" she yelped, her hand covering her heart. Scowling at him, she demanded, "Whatever are you doing? You nearly scared me to death!"

Overcome with laughter at his joke, Mark guffawed, bent nearly double with mirth. The horse he held didn't even react.

"We aren't twelve," she reminded him acidly. "This is so juvenile!"

Wiping tears from his eyes, he choked out, "You jumped so high!"

Sarah shook her head, glaring at him. "This is what you do here at Gideon's? I thought you were learning to be a blacksmith."

His laughter subsiding to chuckles, he replied, "*Neh*. I just help around the shop. It's a busy place. You know, bring the horses—like this one—in to be shod. The 'smithing part is all Gideon. I gladly leave it to him."

She glowered at him, saying, "Then I'd think you'd want to learn a thing or two, particularly since Gideon's so successful."

Mark stroked a hand over the horse's shoulder, fortunately not spooked by his yelling. "*Neh*. I'm not sure I'm cut out to be a blacksmith."

Her mouth assuming a sour smile, Sarah said, "Not cut out to be a farmer or a blacksmith? What exactly do you think *Gott* has in mind for you to do?"

Not allowing himself to be disturbed by her mocking question, Mark's smile deliberately widened. She was so cute, all blue-eyed and deliciously round in her pale green dress, ruffled up like a little, layer chicken, "I'm not sure, Sarah Beiler. You will certainly be a wonderful *Frau* and *Mamm*, when you decide who to marry, but we sad *Menner* have to decide the best path."

She looked at him suspiciously, as if not sure whether he were joking with her.

"I doubt you'll ever pick a work path."

"What do you mean?" he asked, the smile finally slipping from his face at this sarcastic statement.

Again, chiding herself for venturing to comment about what was admittedly no business of hers, Sarah knew she should hush, but he annoyed her, not seeming to see how his behavior affected his life.

"Just that you act like a *Schmetterling*, flitting from job to job. Will you never settle into one work and make a home for a *familye*?"

Mark's laugh now was hard, the tall blond *Mann* looking more irritated than Sarah had ever seen him. She lifted her chin, refusing to back down.

"You should think about how you represent *Gott's* love with your tongue, Sarah. I'm nothing like a butterfly," he said. "Do you see wings on my shoulders? *Schmetterling* are *Gott's* work. They draw attention to His glory. As you know, we are plain and simple."

Impatiently, she waved a dismissive hand. "I only meant that to say how you move from work to work. Of course, you don't have wings."

"Knowing the best way we can act in *Gott's* service requires thought," was his lofty defense. "And I'll pick my work before you'll choose a husband. Are you courting with any of the *Menner*? You left school last year, but you've not yet settled down yourself."

Recoiling from his angry words, she shot back, "Don't be silly. The two are not the same. And besides, considering a life mate is important!"

"As is a *Mann* considering his life work!"

She'd never seen him this angry, but Sarah ignored the little voice in her head that told her to end this. "A *Maedel* will never change her husband, but a *Mann* can change his work. Even serious work, if he has to. Think of your *Bruder*, Jesse. He's had two jobs that will keep his *familye* safe, only changing this when bringing his *Kinder* back home to loving relatives after his *Frau* died."

"Jesse could have stayed on their farm there," Mark retorted. "He told me this. He returned here for himself—and we're very glad he did—as well as for the *Kinder*."

"Jesse—and *Menner* like him—will always provide for his *familye*!" Her face felt flushed.

"From what I see, you are the *Schmetterling*, Sarah, flitting from *Mann* to *Mann*. In the months I worked on Enoch's farm, no *Menner* came to court you. *Yah*, you let them drive you home from Sings, but this never goes anywhere. If you're not careful, Sarah, you'll end up a spinster!"

She gasped. "You are *Verrickt*! I know *Menner*! Both in school and now at Sings. I will marry when I find the right *Mann*! Not one like you who will leave his *Kinder* penniless if he dies, dependent on others to care for them!"

"And I," Mark shot back, "will settle into a job when I find the right one for me! *Maedels* cannot understand this process. Why, I'll bet that I do this soon and definitely before you find a husband."

"That is a silly thing to say!" She knew her face was red, but this *Mann* made her so angry.

"Silly or not, I say it will be that way. I will settle into one work before you choose a *Mann* to marry."

"You are wrong, Mark Fisher," she snapped. "The way you're going, I will be a *Frau* with many *Kinder* and you still will not have work to make you a *gut Daed*!"

CHAPTER FOUR

"Here, Hagar," Sarah said several days later with a sympathetic smile. "I picked this remedy up from *Frau* Miller, telling her you needed something for being in the family way. She's so good with herbs and such."

"*Denki*," Hagar responded, taking the bottle Sarah handed her. "Mercy is such a blessing."

She looked both pale and tired. Sarah hoped having *Bopplin* didn't take her this way.

"Even the twins didn't come this hard at the beginning," Hagar said with an eye roll. "I believe this *Boppli* will be very strong-willed. Of course, I am a little older than when Anna and James were born, but *Gott* is with me and the *Boppli*."

Giving a soft laugh, Sarah patted her shoulder. "*Yah*, He is. You are not so old, not as old as Biblical Sarah was when she gave birth to Isaac. *Gott* knows what we don't."

"This is true." Hagar's smile was accepting.

"Can I do anything for you while I'm here?"

"Hmm. You could start supper, I suppose. Gideon and young Esther have been very helpful—even the twins help out, of course."

"Of course, I can help Esther start supper. We don't want Gideon to have to leave the forge early to do this. Not with him having only Mark to help him," she finished, her words having an edge.

Even though she wasn't at full strength, Hagar laughed. "Oh, Mark has been very helpful. Gideon tells me all the things he's done every day. Mark even came up with a way to better bring horses into the 'smithy, Gideon said. Something about them being calmer if tied to the fence around the outside pen and then walked peacefully into the 'smithy. Mark seems to have *gut* ideas."

"Oh." Sarah bit her tongue. Mark certainly never had a peaceful effect on her, although his intelligence could never be doubted. It peeved her—probably more than it should—that he didn't use his head to make a settled life for himself. "He's very *Schmaert.*"

"*Yah.*" Hagar leaned her head against the rocker's high back.

Nine-year-old Esther marched in, looking competent and business-like, a black *Kapp* perched on her head. She patted her *Mamm's* hand. "Are you feeling any better?"

"A little," Hagar murmured.

"Can I help you start supper?" Sarah offered, very aware of not taking over. Esther was stepping forward to help with her *familye*. Sarah had done the same for her *Mamm* when Kate didn't feel well.

"*Denki,*" Esther responded, shifting a bowl over. "Perhaps you could peel the potatoes."

"Of course." She capably tied an apron around her waist and set to skinning the potatoes. "Dice them up into this bowl?"

"Yes, that would be great," responded Esther, stirring a pan on the stove.

"You're sure Kate doesn't need you?" asked Hagar, glancing at the child.

"*Neh*, my *Geschwischder* are helping. Even though Joshua is only eight and Matthew even younger, they're very determined to help." Sarah grinned over her shoulder. "Elizabeth is *gut* at helping them help without them knowing this."

The kitchen door opened just then and Gideon swept in with Mark trailing him.

Feeling herself tighten at his presence, she made sure to keep steadily peeling the potatoes. It made no sense to care if Mark were here. He'd been in their kitchen at home many times.

Of course, the two of them had not long ago had that silly conversation when he claimed he'd find a permanent job before she chose a husband. How ridiculous!

The big farrier paused, squatting beside his *Frau* to hold her hand and engage in a murmuring conversation with Hagar.

"No! You can't have a taste!" Laughing, young Esther swatted at Mark's hand as he stopped beside her at the stove.

Sarah looked back at the potatoes she was peeling and cutting into chunks, aware that her skin had gotten hotter for some reason. She hated that this uncommitted, unruly *Mann* affected her in any way. As he was very much not in her definition of husband-material, she shouldn't even have noticed him. It made no sense that her ears perked up at the deeper sound of his voice, her side vision reporting faithfully how he teased with the young *Maedel* at the stove.

Drawing a deep breath, her mouth quirked to one side as she replayed Mark's insulting claim that he'd settle into a career before she married. Up until that point, she thought merely that it was a waste that such an upstanding *Mann* was so unfocused. Now, that he'd made his silly bet with her, she was self-conscious, worrying that she hadn't yet started courting seriously with any one of the *Menner* thereabout.

It had several times flashed through her mind that she was headed toward using a matchmaker to find herself a husband. Distressing thought as she was only eighteen.

Acutely conscious that Mark had come over to stand at her shoulder, she kept her eyes on the bowl of potatoes in front of her.

"You're making dinner here tonight? I had no idea." Mark grinned as he spoke in a lowered voice. "I remember you and Kate and your *Schweschder* Elizabeth making potato pies. Yum."

"Perhaps I should stay to have my supper here, Gideon," he called out. "They won't miss me at home."

Straightening from his spot, Gideon laughed. "I don't know what we're having, but you're welcomed to stay."

"I think you're silly," Anna announced to Mark the next day.

"What do you mean?" he asked, his brows lifted in exaggerated surprise.

"You're just silly," the seven-year-old decreed with a wave of her hand. "You say silly things."

"I don't know what you mean," he responded in a sad voice. "I just asked if you and your *Geschwischder* had named the hens in the hen house. My twin and I named all our chickens when we were your age. They have different personalities, you know. Hens. Grace and I noticed that right away when we fed ours. Some hurry up to gobble down the grain and some are choosier, walking around clucking first. They're just different."

The two sat on a log that helped define the buggy parking area outside Gideon's forge.

"That's what I mean," Anna said with a severity that seemed funny on her young face. "How do you expect a *Maedel* like Sarah to take you seriously, if you're so silly all the time?"

"What makes you think I want Sarah to take me seriously?"

"Well, you like her," the girl said, her expression severe. "I mean that's obvious."

Mark had never thought he was easily read. Most of the time, he was told his face didn't give away much.

Her twin, young James, then ambled out of his *Daed's* forge and sat on the log with them.

"What are you two talking about?"

"That Sarah will never like Mark seriously," the girl said, "if he doesn't act less silly."

"Oh." James didn't seem to question his twin's assessment or have an issue with the subject she'd disclosed.

Mark chuckled. It was interesting to see the twin bond between the two. He completely felt the same with Grace, his own twin.

At the same time, Anna's awareness that he liked Sarah was a little disturbing. He did like Sarah—a lot, actually—but that didn't mean he was ready for her to know it. Or anyone, for that matter.

Sarah annoyed him. Attracted him, bossy, sassy *Maedel* that she was.

He liked her sharp comebacks and the way she laughed when he said something to amuse her. He liked her smile.

"If you like her," Anna went on, "you need to show her that. You know, act like she's special. Bring her things. Tell her you like her cooking and the breads she makes."

Mark looked down at the girl, the corner of his mouth quivering despite his attempt to present a serious face. It was amusing to have a seven-year-old coach him in the area of love.

"Tell me, young Anna, what do you think *Maedels* want in the *Mann* they court?"

"They want someone to do the slaughtering," James chimed in, presenting a practical perspective.

"*Yah*," agreed his loyal sister, "but I know that our *Daed* is kind to *Mamm*. Well, to all of us."

"Kind." Mark nodded, schooling his face to reflect attention.

"He hugs her and I've seen them kiss," James offered, looking a little embarrassed.

Anna agreed. "There is hugging and kissing, but I think that must wait until one's married."

"Oh, yes." James picked up a stick and started dragging it along the mud beside the log.

"I don't think I should hug or kiss Sarah, at this point." Mark couldn't help grinning.

"*Neh*," Anna looked severe again, "but girls also want a *Buwe* who doesn't tease them or throw frogs at them."

That made Mark laugh outright. "I can swear to never throw a frog at Sarah."

"I've also heard her tell *Mamm* one time that she wants a *Mann* who will take care of her and their *Kinner*."

"*Daeds* take care of *Kinner*," James said.

"Not all *Daeds*," Anna interjected. "My friend, Abigail, had to move in with her *Grossdaddi* last year because her *Daed* and *Mamm* couldn't afford to get a *Haus*. They moved to another town."

Her twin nodded again. "Our *Daed* has talked to me about making sure I learn a trade."

This sobered Mark. Sarah had been very clear about the subject in her sassy comments. He hadn't thought much about this, despite the bet he'd made with her.

The *Maedel* brought out the worst in him, undoubtedly, but her fixation on his job made no sense to him.

A week later, Jesse stood on his back porch, looking out at the gloomy early morning, a fine mist falling all around. The dampness made the place smell sweeter somehow, the summer dust settled and green growing things seeming to sigh in the moisture. There were times he missed farming and this was one of them.

A wave a sadness streaked across his mind and Jesse shook it away, refusing to dwell on things past. Working in the store was new to him, but he found a strange comfort in marking lists of the items that needed ordering and keeping his figures straight.

Just now, a slight movement near the hen house in the watery dawn light drew his gaze and Jesse frowned, trying to make it out.

He'd grown up on a farm—as well as keeping the one he and Hannah bought back in Montegue—and he knew the damage both foxes and other predators could wreck. As a boy, he'd once chased an owl trying to fly off with a hen. Jesse would never forget the hen's startled squawk when the rock he'd awkwardly thrown had miraculously connected with the ravening owl and scared it into dropping the hen.

Peering through the dim, gloomy light, he saw a slight figure stepping out of the hen house, a basket hung over one arm. He could just make out Anna, her *Kapp* pale white in the dimness.

As she turned and made her way toward the kitchen porch through the mist, he found himself gravitating toward the porch steps, as if to meet her.

Her steps sounded on the wooden steps before she looked up to see him, a smile breaking over her features. "*Goedemorgen!*" "You weren't in the kitchen," he observed neutrally. "Just the *Kinner*, eating their porridge. Don't you have things to do to help your *Mamm*? We don't want to steal you away from her."

Anna smiled before responding, "I'm doing my chores there before I come over. *Mamm* and I wake up early. It's not like we keep a full farm either, just a few hens and some housework. *Mamm* likes doing the cooking, so I'm just in her way in the kitchen."

The warm way she said this made him respond. "You and your *Mamm* are close, aren't you? I mean more even than most *Kinder* and their *Eldre*."

"I suppose so. Since my *Daed* died and we moved here, it's just been the two of us. *Mamm* and *Daed* were never blessed with other *Kinner*."

He hitched his suspenders up on his shoulders more securely, musing not for the first time that Anna was a gentle soul. She was shy, but she lit up when talking comfortably about matters important to her.

The dawn light was soft as it crept into the yard and this conversation seemed comfortable. "Surely you have *familye* here?" he said. "You moved here after your *Daed's* death when there were other places."

"Oh, yes. *Mamm* has several older sisters here and then we realized we're related to Kate Miller."

His gaze dropped to the basket she held. "You mustn't let Joel and Levi talk you into doing their chores. All need to do their part."

"*Yah*," she said, switching her egg-laden basket to her other hand.

"They could have brought in the eggs."

"I know," Anna responded with an open smile, "even little Eve is learning to do this, but it's so wet this morning—and they were so hungry."

Adjusting his suspenders on his shoulders, Jesse couldn't help responding to her with a faint smile. "You mustn't spoil them, you know. A little wet won't hurt them."

"*Neh*, or me, either." She swiped a hand across a damp cheek. "This was just a little treat. The boys both have already made their beds, swept their room and the kitchen, plus made up the fire in the stove."

She met his gaze. "Did you eat? I can see you're heading into the store early."

"*Yah*, I hope to get some work done before the customers arrive." Jesse positioned his hat on his head. "And, yes, I had porridge and some of the eggs you made."

Anna noticed then that he carried nothing.

"Did you not see the lunch I made for you? You need to take something to eat."

"*Neh*," he said slowly before adding, "you spoil us, Anna. I asked you only to watch over the *Kinder* for me and here you are gathering eggs in the rain and making my lunch."

She could feel herself blushing, hurrying to say. "I don't mind! I like doing these things."

He wasn't to know that she felt more right here, taking care of the *Kinner* and the house—taking care of him, if she was honest with herself—than she felt in any other spot right now. It would never do to let him see how she felt. To be honest, she was embarrassed to feel this way for any *Mann*. It didn't seem that she had the right, given her record with *Menner*.

"Why don't—" Jesse broke off, turning to look up the steps he'd started descending, looking a little self-conscious. "Why don't you bring me my lunch later? You and the *Kinder*, of course. It will be a nice break in the day for me."

She felt herself flushing with pleasure at the suggestion. "That—that would be very nice. The children will like that. They miss you."

He smiled up at her and Anna suddenly saw a before-unrealized resemblance to his audacious *Bruder*. "That's kind of you to say. Okay, then, I'll just head off to the store."

Anna didn't know what emboldened her to blurt out. "I know this must be difficult for you. Moving your *familye* here, running the store…all with having lost your *Frau*."

Half expecting him to stiffen into the remote *Mann* he'd been at the first, she held her breath, mentally berating herself for having said anything.

"*Neh*," he said soberly from the bottom of the porch steps. "This was hardest for the *Kinder*, particularly with having lost their *Mamm* so recently."

Coming closer to the steps, Anna said softly, "I can't imagine."

The bad times of her life had been when Hiram, her now-deceased husband, had left her and their life here. It embarrassed her a little to admit that losing her *Mamm* would be harder than having lost her husband.

"It was hard for them." As he bent his head then, his hat hid his face from her.

"Harder for you," she said warmly. Her marriage to Hiram hadn't been happy, as mortifying as it was for him to leave her. She recognized that she didn't know the deep sadness of losing a beloved mate. She'd heard all about Jesse's loving marriage from her more direct friend, Sarah. "Hannah was your beloved *Frau*."

He lifted his head then, his sigh short. "Yes, she was, but I must go forward now. Take care of the *Kinder*."

Anna felt the world tilt a little as she stared into his eyes, dimly aware that she was glad she could help by providing loving, kind care to his children. She felt the crimson flush in her cheeks again. "It would be nice to—for us all to see you in the middle of the day. I will bring you lunch later."

"This is a good patch!" Elizabeth yelled, waist-deep in blueberries two weeks later.

Sarah laughed at the sight of her younger sister, the girl's black *Kapp* bobbing through the patch as she bent to pick the clusters of berry fruit off the stems.

"Such enthusiasm," Anna commented with a gentle laugh.

Reaching out to clasp her friend's forearm above where a fruit basket dangled, Sarah said, "I'm so glad your *Mamm* could spare you to come with us. I'm sure she likes you being home when you're not watching Jesse's *Kinner*."

"She does, indeed," Anna agreed, walking in the row of squatty bushes next to Sarah. "She likes me having work, though."

"How is it going?" Sarah reached to pluck the clusters of plump berries as they made their way toward young Elizabeth. "Jesse said he's very grateful to have you with the children. It's been nice, too, that you bring them to the store to see him for lunch. He's a nice *Mann*, isn't he?"

"*Yah*," Anna agreed. "Don't you think he and Mark look alike? They have the same smile."

"Maybe," agreed Sarah, her annoyance rising at the thought of tall, attractive, but very annoying Mark. How could one *Mann* be so dense? "That is to be expected with them being *Bruders*."

"But they're so different," her friend said in her soft voice as she picked blueberries from the other side of the row of plants. "Mark is always teasing and joking where Jesse has seen hardship."

"He's known sadness, for sure, what with his wife dying," Sarah responded before her mouth twisted as she said, "but Mark is definitely not always laughing. I mean, he seems like he's joking most of the time—even when he's being mean."

Anna looked over at her. "What are you saying? He's been mean to you?"

"Nothing," Sarah muttered, suddenly wishing her unruly tongue would stay quiet. She didn't want to discuss Mark's statements about her with anyone. Not even Anna. It was embarrassing. "The two *Bruders* are very different, that's all. Even though they look a little alike."

"Oh." Anna gave her an intent look before saying. "I'm enjoying looking after Jesse's *Kinner*. Such lovely children."

"You should come over here!" Elizabeth shouted from her spot several rows away. "There are so many blueberries!"

"I think this whole patch is *gut*!" Sarah called back to her.

Anna shook her head with a chuckle. "That Joel, though, can be quite a handful. I prefer the *Kinner* like that, though, as they all seem more natural than when I first started caring for them. More normal and not so stricken."

Sarah made a face at her. "A handful?"

"Just *Kinner*. Nothing meanspirited. I found him and Levi all covered in mud one afternoon when they were supposed to be weeding the kitchen garden. They'd gotten in a 'weed-fight,' they said. Those weeds must have had a lot of dirt on their roots."

Her friend laughed softly before she went on. "They were filthy dirty!"

Picking fat, ripe blueberries as she made her way down the row, Sarah said, "Marrying an older, settled *Mann* would be *gut*, I suppose. Naturally, he would have children."

"Naturally," Anna responded after a minute, bending to pull berries from a bush.

Her muted response drew Sarah's gaze. How could she have forgotten Anna's unique situation? She and heartless Hiram had been blessed with no children. Given Hiram's subsequent behavior, that was probably for the best. Still, here Anna was—no husband, no *Kinder* to comfort her. Unfairly tarnished in the eyes of many.

"You would have made a wonderful *Mamm*. You will be a wonderful *Mamm* one day," Sarah said in a stout voice.

Anna smiled at her. "Thank you for that. I'm so glad you're my friend."

"I would think," Sarah said, continuing pulling blueberries off and placing them in her fruit basket, "that caring for Jesse's *Kinder* will show that to anyone who might wonder."

"Possibly."

"It is a good thing, Anna," Sarah turned back to say earnestly to her friend, "that you had no children with Hiram. Consider how messy everything would have been, what with him leaving for the *Englischer* world and then getting killed in that fight."

"*Kinner* are a gift from *Gott*," her friend responded, her soft voice flat. "No matter what the situation."

Continuing to harvest blueberries, Sarah mused, "*Yah*. I suppose if you had *Kinner*, the elders and Bishop might have felt more need to find you a husband after Hiram died."

"Maybe," a smile glimmered on Anna's lips, "but now I'm free to watch Jesse's children... and they deserve *gut* care. Their father also deserves to have help in that way."

Sarah paused, lifting her skirt to scratch her leg. "Jesse is a nice *Mann*. If only Mark were more like him! The careless, heedless *Mann*! More *Buwe* than *Mann*, him."

Anna sent her a laughing look, "Not heedless, just not as settled yet. He's nice. I like him. Give him time, Sarah."

"Jesse can, at least, provide for his *Kinner*!" Sarah knew her animated response was more intense than the situation called for, but Mark's actions irritated her too much to ignore.

It seemed like such a waste! If he were not so unmindful of his future, Mark would be a very attractive husband for any *Maedel*. Sarah brooded on the thought. Even as thoughtless as her tongue could be, she knew she couldn't take him aside and give him a serious talking-to.

As it was, she'd probably said too much to him.

With a deep sigh, she promised to mind her own business more. Mark wasn't her concern, after all. She just needed to find the right *Mann* for her.

A settled, focused, responsible husband who would never leave his *familye* not provided for. It shouldn't be too hard.

She released another gusty sigh, faintly depressed even though she shouldn't be.

"You like Mark," Anna said with a smile. "I think you should admit it to yourself."

"I don't know what you mean," Sarah snapped, "and you just said you liked him yourself."

Her friend's smile widened. "I think you do know what I mean."

Continuing down the row of blueberry bushes, Sarah called out to Elizabeth, using this as an excuse to keep from responding. Looking back at the dark leaves of the bush in front of her, she finally said as calmly as she could, "Mark is a very nice *Mann*. Everyone likes him."

This was depressingly true.

Anna laughed. "I mean—which you know very well—that you more than like him."

"I like a lot of *Menner*," Sarah responded loftily, "that doesn't mean I want to marry them or think they'd make *gut* husbands."

When her friend giggled, she added. "*Gott* recommends us not to judge our brethren, but we must carefully select our mates."

"*Yah*, He does recommend we not judge others as we know not the heart."

"I'm not sure," Sarah admitted ruefully "that I even know my own heart. Not really."

Laughing again, Anna said, "Well, you can be certain that *Gott* does. Just pray that you hear always His word."

Several minutes went by before Sarah responded with a burst of honesty. "Do you think *Gott* tried to warn you not to marry Hiram? And you somehow didn't listen?"

Shaking her head, Anna's smile faded away as she considered the question. "I don't know. We cannot know *Gott's* ways. These are sometimes too big for our little minds. I know He loves me—and that He loved Hiram. As to His plan for me, I have spoken to the Bishop about it. I cannot know that, but I believe it will be revealed one day."

Sarah waited as Anna drew near, her sympathy for her friend nearly choking her. "You are a very *gut* girl. Many would have lost their faith, going through all you have. I probably would have."

Her friend shook her head, continuing to pull fat blueberries to fill her basket. "You don't give yourself enough credit, but I think that's a problem for you with Mark, as well."

Sarah turned back to the blueberry bushes as they neared the end of a row.

With a deep sigh, she considered Mark again. "He is fun and he is nice to look at. I just worry that he'll never be the kind of *Mann* on which a *Maedel* can rely."

"You worry about that?" Anna said, her smile a glimmer again.

"*Yah*, but I need to stop dwelling on his journey," Sarah declared resolutely, "and pick a *Mann* with whom to court. That's what I need to do."

"Best wishes with that," Anna responded in her soft voice.

CHAPTER FIVE

"You always seem so...so calm and nice during our worship meetings," Sarah told Mark the Monday after their next Sunday service. Noting with frustration that her words sounded a tad schoolteacher-prudish, she cringed inside. She'd wanted to sound casual and disinterested.

Working now in Jesse's store, Sarah was in the middle of wiping down the front counter before they opened for the morning.

Mark looked up from measuring a shelving unit across the way, saying with amusement, "As opposed to my usual—being all frantic and mean?"

She chuckled, shrugging. "You know what I'm saying. What are you doing here? Aren't you supposed to be working with Gideon at the forge?"

"I've finished there," Mark said, not looking up from his measurement notes. "Jesse asked me to build some extra shelves for the store before I go to work with Josiah and Leah on their farm next week."

"What?" She craned her neck around to look at him.

"*Yah.* Josiah wrote a letter to Gideon, mentioning that he and Luke need some help there. You know Josiah apprenticed a while at Gideon's forge?"

"Of course. That's how he and Leah met again and later married," she responded, her tone sharper than she'd intended. "But that was years ago."

Mark looked up. "Yes, and Gideon and Josiah apparently stayed friends."

"So, you're no longer working with Gideon and now you're moving where? To Windber? To Leah and Josiah's farm," she snapped with a surge of irritation, not sure why she was surprised. She wasn't sure why this news upset and angered her, but her heart was suddenly pounding with both.

Mark looked up from writing his measurements on a pad. "*Yah.* I'm moving for a while to Windber. I probably won't be there long—"

"No doubt!" she said, the words tart.

"Sarah." Jesse came out of the back office. "You can unlock the doors now and flip the sign."

"Oh, yes. It's time, isn't it?" She dropped her cleaning rag to hurry to the door.

"And I'll handle the customers for now. I want you to help Mark with the shelves that he's building.

She looked up quickly as she walked back to continue cleaning.

"It seems we're always being directed to work together again," Mark said, in a voice only she could hear.

"Of course, Jesse," she said automatically, irritated that she wasn't more annoyed to be assigned this.

"He will be putting these long boards together," Jesse went on, oblivious. "He'll need your help."

"At least, it's not a cistern." Laughter trembled in Mark's quiet words.

Frowning—and ashamed that she didn't mind working with Mark—she told him severely. "I would think you could manage to make a shelving unit without assistance."

His disregard of responsibility and his reluctance to settle down made her enjoyment of his company all the more frustrating to Sarah.

He laughed. "*Yah,* I can manage the shelves without assistance, but it'll be much easier with you to hold the long boards."

"I must put away the rag," she said readily. "Then I can help."

The bell on the front door she'd just unlocked jangled then as a customer came into the building, but focused on working with Mark, she didn't attend to this.

When Sarah came back from storing her cleaning supplies, she ran across Timothy Musselman, who she'd seen in the store with Hannah Oberli weeks earlier.

"*Hallo*," she greeted Timothy, headed back to work on the shelves with Mark.

"*Hallo*, Sarah. How are you?" Timothy responded cheerfully, stopping as if he'd come into the store just to see her.

His gaze was so intent and his smile so focused on her that Sarah stopped. This time, Timothy was alone. Hannah Oberli and her *Mamm* not in sight.

"The work here is to your liking?" He shifted slightly, as if positioning himself more firmly in her path.

"It is," she responded, noting a determination and deliberation in the way he looked at her. "I like it fine. I was just about to help Mark with a shelving unit he's building."

Timothy glanced over in the direction she'd nodded. "*Yah*, I'm sure you can help with many things here."

Several things registered in her brain at the same moment— Timothy was single, had recently joined the church and was of an age to marry. They also had carried on a minor flirtation in past years.

Rapidly following this, it occurred to her that it wouldn't do Mark Fisher any harm to observe another *Mann's* interest in her.

This might not have been the most admirable action, but it was one that women had employed for eons. She didn't delve into why she wanted him to see this, only that here was an opportunity.

With this plan, Sarah smiled at Timothy more widely and readily than before.

"I saw you at church sitting with Able and Joshua. You've just joined the church, haven't you?"

It went without saying that once a *Mann* had chosen to commit himself to follow the *Ordnung*, he was ready to take a wife.

"*Yah*," Timothy responded, sidling a little closer to her. "I saw you there as well. You, your *Schweschders* and your *Mamm*. You all look to be in very *gut* health."

She'd always liked Timothy, she reminded herself. "We are all well. *Denki*. Is your *familye* doing fine? I believe I saw your *Eldre* at services, as well."

"*Yah*, we were all there." He smiled and nodded.

Was this what it was like to court with a *Mann*, she wondered. Stilted and awkward. Timothy and she had always had an easy-going friendship before. Aware that he worked just steps away from them, Sarah hoped Mark was so riddled with jealousy that he hadn't noticed the strained nature of her interaction with Timothy.

The way Mark's mouth quirked up on one side didn't encourage this wish.

"My *Mamm* has been planning on visiting with yours. Might you both be home someday this next week?"

She shifted to put her back to Mark, by this time, regretting the impulse that had led her in this direction. She had no real interest in Mark. Why should she care what he thought? "*Yah*, I believe so. That is, I'm not exactly sure what *Mamm* has planned."

The rest of her brief conversation with Timothy was a blur to Sarah. She remembered smiling and nodding, while trying to end their interaction quickly. It wasn't that she didn't like him, she assured herself, or that he didn't fit her requirements for a husband. It was only that this didn't seem like an encounter that needed to happen in public.

Certainly not under Mark's mocking gaze. Sarah didn't know why she assumed he'd be mocking about this. Mark just always seemed sarcastic.

"Okay," she assured her possible-beau, now several feet down the aisle, "I'll see you soon."

After Timothy took a few minutes to say his goodbyes, she turned back to where Mark worked. "I'm ready now. What would you like me to do?"

"Here," he responded with just a glimmer of a smile, "hold this."

As he planed smooth the boards that she placed on the sawhorses for him—measuring again and making small marks with an awl and hammer before he took out a hand saw to cut them, Sarah noted how precisely Mark worked. She'd observed this with his work on her *Daed's* farm. Having high requirements of himself was clearly Mark's tendency.

Perhaps this was his reputation and the reason he apparently had no problem finding work.

"Hold this," he instructed, positioning a board as his *Bruder* walked by, attending to the business of the store.

Absently, she braced the shelf, her gaze on Jesse.

Mark shifted the board she'd just laid across the sawhorses. "This one's warped and has a knothole near the end. Get me another board."

"Picky. Picky. Picky," she said in a soft undertone.

"Have you not heard, *Maedel?*" Mark responded with lifted brows, his expression deadpan, "that anything worth doing is worth doing well?"

"An *Englischer* saying," she shot back.

"*Englischers* have some things right. Not many, but some."

"I can see," she said, placing another shelf board on the sawhorses, "that you'll require your *Frau* to be perfect."

He just smiled.

"The *Kinner* will never be dirty or play in the mud. Your *Frau* must keep the *Haus* very, very clean and even the chickens must be kept very neat."

"Don't forget the goats," Mark said with a smile as he shifted the new board to where he could cut it. "They must be free of mud, too, all brushed and neat every day."

Sarah shook her head. "You will be looking for a *Frau* for a very long time then."

He laughed.

Changing the subject, she said, "I hope Anna is caring well for Joel, Levi and Eve."

In working with the *Mann*, she knew that, unlike his attractive *Bruder*, Jesse was a steady provider.

"I think so," Mark responded, glancing up at his older brother. "*Yah.* They actually seem happier when I've seen them since their *Mamm* died. Jesse, too. My *Eldre* are very glad of this."

"*Gut.* Jesse deserves to have some good in his life," she said warmly. She was glad they all saw Anna's value. "It's hard on the *Kinder,* but hard on their *Daed,* as well."

Out of the side of his eye, Mark caught the speculative look Sarah sent Jesse. A shiver of awareness went through him.

"You seem very interested in your boss's well-being." Introspection had never been very important to Mark, but even he noted the oddness of her remark. After all, he had no real interest in who Jesse married next. What if it was Sarah?

He looked down at the board he was marking, suddenly seeing only her fresh-faced smile.

"Of course, I wish good for all," Sarah responded primly. "I'm glad Anna is being of service to the *familye.* She is a *gut* girl and she deserves to be valued."

Mark adjusted his measuring tape. He'd heard about Anna Lehmann Hershberger's burdens. Who in their small town hadn't? Abandoned by her husband, Hiram, who later died in an *Englisher* bar brawl. She didn't deserve any of what had happened to her, in his eyes, but he knew some in their congregation still considered her marked by all that had happened. "She does deserve to be appreciated. Jesse's children seem to really love her."

"*Yah.*" Sarah smiled. "I am so glad."

"You've been a good friend to her."

"Maybe, but she's been just as good a friend to me." She retrieved another board from the pile.

He looked down, noting that Sarah didn't seem to make a big deal of her own actions. She was kind-hearted, even if she was sassy and hasty sometimes.

"It's sad that her *Mamm* and *Daed* had only the one *Kinder,*" he commented "I'd think Anna would have liked having *Geschwischder.* It's a good thing she's got a friend like you."

Sarah laughed. "I'm the lucky one. Anna's like a sister to me. Elizabeth is wonderful, but she's much younger than me. Of course, we still have fun. Just the other day, Anna and Elizabeth and I picked blueberries together."

"Anna is older than you?"

"Only by a few years. Not enough to matter."

"I guess after being an only child yourself for so long," he commented, "finally having both a friend, who is like an older sister, and younger *Geschwischder* must have been nice."

She sent him a sideways look. "*Yah.* I was very glad to have *Mamm* marry Enoch when I got to know him. He's very reserved at first, but *Daed* helped *Mamm* and me when we weren't sure where else we would go."

"You would have been cared for, though. The church people and the bishops would have made sure of that."

Sarah's snort brought his head up and Mark lifted his brows in question.

"Old Bishop Yoder wanted *Mamm* to marry his *Youngie* son, Aaron. I heard *Mamm* and *Daed* discussing it one time. Of course, Aaron Yoder isn't so young now, but back then, he was just a *Buwe.*"

Frowning, Mark tried to remember the particulars of Kate Bieler's widowhood. "Some marry young."

"*Yah,*" she retorted, "but they don't marry a woman who is several years older and brings a child—someone else's child—with her. It's just good Enoch and Kate already loved one another."

Mark knew that Sarah wasn't Kate's child, the girl's own mother having died before Kate married Sarah's father.

Sarah looked somber, as if she, too, were thinking of the dilemma that Kate had faced.

Glancing up to meet his gaze, she abruptly said, "At least, Jesse is doing what's best for his *Kinder.* Looking after them and making sure they're safe."

"*Yah.*" Mark glanced at her, not sure what her comment meant. "Jesse is like that."

"I know," she said, her voice getting stronger. "He stays in one place—unless trying to find a better life—and provides for his *Kinder.*"

The look that accompanied her remark confused him. "What do you mean?"

Sarah snorted. "Only what I've said before, that a *Mann* without steady work is a hazard for the children and for his *Frau*."

"I suppose." He still didn't know what had riled her up suddenly.

"Then why do you drift from job to job?" Her question was harsh. "You would be a great risk for a *Maedel*!"

"Possibly, if I were married, but I'm not. I don't have *Kinder* or a *Frau*," he responded, his voice flat. He knew she had returned to her previous judgement of him. "No one is hurt by my taking different jobs."

"And that is a *gut* thing, although it does mean you aren't doing as *Gott* intended. Didn't He recommend us to marry and bring forth *Kinder* into this world for ours and His joy?"

As much to defend her attack on him as to tease her about her own choices, Mark replied, "I don't see you doing either. No husband. No *Kinder*."

"I'm only eighteen-years-old!" she retorted, her burst of temper seeming to recede.

"And I'm only nineteen." He blew wood particles off the board he'd just finished sawing. "We've both finished with school and no longer in our running around time."

"I did my *rumspringa* last year," she replied in what seemed like an automatic manner.

"And joined the church?"

"I will do that soon," she said defensively.

"And then will be your time to marry."

"I am very aware of that," she shot back. "I wonder how many jobs you will have had by that time!"

"Ten. Maybe twenty." His lips twisted in a version of his smile. Mark couldn't help it. Something about her made him want to rile her up. It was ridiculous to let himself get into this. He didn't particularly like her being mad at him—although he liked being able to provoke her. It made no sense, so he didn't waste time thinking about it. He had no doubt of what she claimed about *Kinder*.

"Rest assured, Sarah. When I choose, I will take care of my *familye* very well and will create no *familye* until then."

Several days later, Bishop Schrock came to visit. Jesse sat on a chair in his austere, practically-furnished living room, staring at the bishop on the couch opposite him.

Jesse cleared his throat. "I'm glad you've come to visit, Bishop. My hometown has been very welcoming. I appreciate your hospitality."

"*Yah.*" Bishop Schrock nodded. "Your *Kinder* are settling in here? You have found someone to care for them until they have a *Mamm*?"

"*Yah.* Although, I—I have not thought to remarry, at this time. My *Frau* only died just a little over a year ago. I'm just trying to get the store running smoothly.

"I understand," the bishop said, his face austere, "but we must look to the future, *der suh. Gott* has directed us to be fruitful and multiply. This directs us to marry. There are several fine *Maedels* here who aren't courting with anyone."

Although this was a Sunday between church meetings, the store was closed to honor the day of rest. Otherwise, Jesse wouldn't have been home.

At this timely moment, Anna came through the kitchen back door. Her cheeks were pleasantly flushed from the heat and her hands dirty from the bunch of bristling red beets she held. She looked healthy and happy.

He found himself grinning. She'd clearly just pulled the vegetables from the garden, probably to prepare them for supper. The beets were obviously the product of vigorous plants, their leaves bright and green above the dark red bulbs.

Since the kitchen was open to the living area, her eruption into the room caused both men to swivel toward the door through which she'd come.

"Yes to both questions, Bishop," Jesse said, still smiling. "*Frau* Hershberger is doing a wonderful job with my children and they are settling in well under her care."

The older *Mann's* smile seemed to tighten before fading away. "*Gut.* I'm glad you don't have that distraction from your work. Like I said, there are *Maedels* here to consider."

"*Denki,*" Jesse responded, for some reason even more self-conscious with Anna just in the kitchen.

She certainly had no claim to him, but for some reason, he didn't want her to feel she might lose her job. It occurred to him in a flash of awareness that he might not have worried about this if she were in her fifties and more generously built. None of this should have mattered, though.

"Like I said, Bishop," Jesse said quietly, shifting away from Anna in his seat, "my concern right now is the business. All else must wait until my *familye* is fully settled in here."

"Don't let this matter wait too long," the bishop said, getting to his feet. "Remember what *Gott* has decreed."

Jesse came into the Brugher *Haus* where Sunday service was being held this week, shifting little Eve in his arms as he looked for a seat. Moving through the crowded house as carefully as he could, he looked for open chairs. Finally, a friend motioned him over and he made his way to a row of seats. After sitting down and getting his children settled, he saw that Anna sat in the row ahead of them, several chairs down from him.

As the meeting progressed, several *Menner* giving talks, Jesse felt the comfort of this ritual seep into him. This was home—his *familye* and friends. His belief in *Gott*. These had gotten him through the dark times.

After the service was over, Jesse sat alone for a while, his *Mamm* having taken his hungry *Kinder* to the eating tables.

Pondering the speakers' words, he mused over recommendations that he should take another wife. He hadn't felt ready for this. Not until now, but perhaps he should give his *Kinner* a mother and himself a helpmate. Joel already tended to worry about him, Jesse knew. This was not the young *Buwe's* job. Jesse was to watch after his son.

The row in front of him where Anna sat next to Sarah Miller was the front in this section of the *Haus* and, as such, there was a parade of folk passing in front as they headed to get lunch.

Jesse's gaze rested idly on this stream of passing humanity as he thought about getting himself another wife. It wasn't really that he believed Hannah, the mother of his kids, would have wanted him to remain unmarried. He was clear that she'd want him to do right by their children and to follow *Gott's* directions. He just didn't feel comfortable with many of the *Maedels* he met. His gaze fell on Anna—now sitting alone as Sarah flitted off to greet a friend—and he found a faint smile curving his lips.

He was comfortable with Anna. She was so kind

He and Hannah had known one another all their lives. It was natural that building a life together had seemed right to them. Her death had left him grieving alone in the darkness of night. It gave him a kind of peace now to see Anna watch over his *Kinner* with such kindness.

Just then, two older *Fraus* walked the path in front of his children's caregiver. This, in itself, was to be expected as Anna sat in the row facing the walkway. He recognized the older women as the wives of two *Menner* in the church.

He saw Anna get up, as if to go toward the kitchen where some of the women were preparing and serving lunch for all.

In one very awkward moment that could have easily gone unnoticed, Anna stood waiting for the chatting women to pass. As she was hardly two feet away from them—and they were such a small community as to make all known to one another—it would seem natural for the women to have offered Anna a greeting as they passed. They didn't.

Jesse watched in startled realization as one of the two glanced at Anna, clearly seeing her waiting there for them to pass, but no greeting was given. Jesse was so startled by this open disdain from one church member to another. It was as if the woman and her friend looked right through Anna.

The non-interchange was over in a few seconds. The two went on their way and Anna went off to the kitchen to help, he assumed. The older *Fraus'* snubbing behavior wasn't acknowledged either by themselves or by Anna, and this set Jesse to thinking.

He'd moved away from Mannheim after marrying Hannah, buying a farm near her *familye*. He had known Anna when they were *scholars* in school, but Jesse realized that he knew little about her from school forward. He heard she'd married Hiram Hershberger who had later died somehow. Having been involved in running his farm and building his *familye* with Hannah, he hadn't paid much attention to what had led to Hiram's death.

Maybe all this had nothing to do with the treatment Anna had just faced, but he couldn't help wondering.

Finding his *Kinner* at the eating tables with his *Mamm* and Grace, Jesse found his attention drawn away from the subject. He waited in line to fill his plate and joined them at the tables. In between taking a spoonful of stew and listening to Joel tell him a story, Jesse noted Anna crossing in front of him. Carrying her plate, she went to find a place to sit.

Jesse stared at her a moment. Although she was heaven-sent for his children, he didn't know a lot about her life after he'd moved from Mannheim.

Several minutes later, he saw Anna approaching an empty nearby table with her modest plate of food. He sat now at a table that had cleared out around him, noting that she was heading to a table several feet away.

Overwhelmed by curiosity about her life, Jesse called out. "Anna! Come sit here. My *Mamm* and Grace have my three *Kinder* in hand, leaving me here all alone. It's embarrassing."

He felt natural, teasing with her a little. This was Anna, after all.

She laughed, shifting to make her way to his table. "We can't have that."

They both sat at the table, eating in silence except for the occasional random interaction. When Anna had put down her fork and wiped her mouth on a napkin, Jesse cleared his throat.

"I don't know if you realized it, but the *Kinner* and I sat a row or so behind you during service."

"Oh, no I didn't know."

"My *Mamm* and Grace sat with us." Not exactly sure how to proceed, Jesse fiddled with a crumpled napkin where it sat on his dirty plate.

"I bet the children were happy."

"*Yah*, they were."

No brilliant method to bring up the topic having occurred to him, he decided to plunge in anyway.

Jesse swallowed and then said, "I saw *Frau* Bichsel and *Frau* Yoder walk past you earlier without speaking to you."

"Oh!" She looked self-conscious. "Did they?"

"*Yah*, and they glanced your way, but seemed to deliberately ignore that you were there. Several other older women seemed to do the same." Jesse fell silent, not sure how to proceed."

Anna's napkin lay in a twisted mass on her plate, her nervous fingers having nearly shredded it.

Jesse looked at the table in front of him and then up at her. "It has occurred to me that I know little of your life after I married and left Mannheim."

Looking at him through wide eyes, her mouth trembled a little and she said nothing.

"I know nothing of what happened to you here. You and Hiram Hershberger were married. I heard that."

Anna still said nothing, her eyes seeming to shimmer with what looked like tears. Finally, she offered, "Hiram is dead."

"I know," Jesse said slowly, "but there was—were problems before he died, weren't there? Seems like I heard that he left our life, the church and you?"

Nodding jerkily, she said, "Yes, he did."

Seeing her reaction, he knew the subject was painful for her, but he couldn't let it go.

"He left here and then died?"

"*Yah.* There was a fight in an *Englischer* bar. Hiram was killed in it."

Silence ticked by as Jesse desperately tried to find a good response to this. "*Englischer* bars can be dangerous, I've heard," he said finally.

Anna bent her head. "Some think that Hiram's actions before he died…might have been because of me."

Jesse felt his eyebrows twitch into a frown as she spoke

"Particularly *Eldre*," Anna said in her soft voice, "who fear that their own children will reject *Gott* and meet Hiram's end. This makes it difficult for them to be kind."

"I do not see that you are responsible for Hiram's choices," protested Jesse. "No one directs the actions of another. Even *Gott* has given us choice. We, each one, have that power."

"Do you think you'd see this so clearly if Joel or Levi were to leave the church?"

Jesse looked at her across the table. "Well, no. Not that clearly, anyway, but I hope I'd resist the urge to blame another. I'd be more likely, in that case, to blame myself."

"I suppose that's natural," she responded. "It's still *Kinder* making choices, though. Not the parents. There is tremendous grief, though."

She cleared her throat and blinked before saying in a direct tone, "I should have talked to you about it before you hired me to be with your children. Told you about this. I just thought that with them being so young, maybe my history didn't need to be brought up."

Reaching out a hand impulsively, Jesse covered one of hers with his. "I'm not asking because I think you'll influence my children in a bad way. I just saw those women being…unkind to you and…. I wanted to understand. We've known *Frau* Bichsel and *Frau* Yoder since we were *Youngies*."

Anna drew a deep breath before responding. "*Yah*, we have…and they are *gut* people, both of them."

Jesse's mouth turned up at the corner. "It's surprising to hear you say that when both have been unkind to you."

"I think it's important to remember that parents worry about their children and, particularly in a situation like this, they worry about their children being pulled out of their loving relationship with *Gott,*" she said sadly, "and out of the life He's recommended to us."

"Yes, but you had nothing to do with Hiram leaving after he married you."

Shaking her head sorrowfully, she gazed across the yard outside the Haus and said, "*Neh*, Jesse. My *Mamm* told me that *Eldre* always find it easier to put the blame on someone other than their *Kinder*."

He felt a frown descend onto his face. "Anna, you could not have made Hiram do this. You could not be the reason he left you—his wife—and this life. This isn't something a wife would cause."

"You cannot know," she said in her soft, calm voice. "Maybe I was a terrible wife and he left here, rather than stay married to me."

Her words surprised a short laugh from him. "I do not believe you could ever be so dreadful."

Letting a small smile slip onto her lips, she said, "*Denki*, Jesse. That is nice of you."

"Are the *Menner* in this town blind? I never thought so before. Why has none courted with you?" he asked.

"I am—" she paused for a moment. "I am damaged goods, though. You must see that."

"I still say," he repeated in a staunch voice, "that the *Menner* here have to be fools not to see your kind heart. They've known you from childhood—as have I—and your spirit should be known to them."

"Maybe," she said in a soft voice, "but fear is a strong emotion."

"Are you settled in?" *Frau* Miller smiled at Mark across the table two weeks later.

"*Yah,* very well." Mark smiled widely, reaching for the bowl of cooked green beans to add a spoonful to his plate.

The farm in Windber was rich and Mark's employer, Josiah, well able to employ a crew to help with the harvest and the shoeing of their horses. Mark had only been there two days, but he could see how well Josiah and his farm manager, Luke, ran the place.

"*Mamm,*" *Scholar* Eli asked, "may I have some more potatoes?"

"Of course." Leah Miller took his plate with a smile. "We certainly want you powered up. *Grossdaddi* Luke and your *Daed* want you to help in the fields this afternoon."

"*Yah.*" Josiah wiped his mouth with a napkin. "Even if you just run water to the workers, that will help."

He turned to Mark. "Luke is married to my *Mamm,* you know."

"They love having the *Kinder* around." Leah smiled. "Luke's children—and grandchildren—live so far away."

Accustomed to church members having many connections through marriages, this didn't surprise him.

The back door opened then and several young children came in, their *Mamm* inspecting to see if they'd washed their hands at the pump outside. Mark thought these two *Kinder* were just younger than Eli—Abigail and Adam? He was still learning all their names.

A baby snoozed in the cradle in a warm kitchen alcove and this was little Hannah.

"Are your *Geschwischder* coming in for their lunch?" Leah asked in a stern tone.

Smiling at his plate, Mark could remember his own *Mamm* questioning him about the same thing.

"I don't know," the girl answered in a composed, high-pitched voice, her *Kapp* perched on her blonde head. "I was emptying the water from the hand washer and moving the basket of clothes, as you asked. I wasn't attending to Damaris and Ezekiel. You told them to come in. Maybe they're still playing catch around the yard."

She said this with aplomb, her self-confidence seeming almost comical coming from a child.

He smiled at the thought that Sarah would have been just such a child. He'd not seen her since leaving Gideon and Hagar's farm and he wondered if she'd found a *Mann* with whom to court.

Smile fading, he found he didn't like that idea, at all.

Mark swallowed and took another mouthful, *Frau* Miller's delicious dinner suddenly tasted like sawdust in his mouth. True, he wanted to win the bet he'd laid with her and, at the same time, wasn't about to frame his future at her bidding.

He still didn't like thinking of her with another *Mann*.

As talk shifted around the Miller's full lunch table—the other two small Millers having made their way inside—Mark began considering the *Menner* in Mannheim. These were the obvious choices for Sarah and most of them were Mark's friends. *Yah*, several were already courting with other *Maedels*, but there were those remaining.

He liked them as friends, but he could see none strong enough to stand up to Sarah Bieler. Quiet amidst the chatter flowing around him, he thought of the girl's spunky, bossy ways.

She wasn't easy to forget, but the thought of her needled him uncomfortably. It wasn't any of his business who she eventually married. His bigger concern was settling in here for the time being.

The service several days later having finished, Sarah didn't immediately head to the kitchen to help serve lunch. She'd do this in a few moments, but instead turned to the row of chairs behind her to speak to Hagar and Gideon. As she swiveled around, their twins, Anna and James, hurried out to play with friends before the food was served.

Smiling affectionately after the *Kinder*, she turned toward Hagar. Rounding now from the new child she carried, Hagar sat between her oldest *Dochder*, Esther, and Gideon.

"Those two," she laughed as her twins rushed out.

"I'm still here," Esther reminded her, looking very satisfied when her *Mamm* patted her knee.

"Yes, you are."

"Are you feeling better?" Sarah asked the pregnant woman solicitously.

"*Yah*," Hagar responded with a chuckle. "Thanks to Mercy's elixir and time."

"*Gut*." Sarah added without thinking, "It's probably easier now that you have one less mouth at dinner time."

Hagar said, "What?"

Feeling self-conscious in spite of herself, she clarified, "I'm sure you have less to do since Mark no longer works with Gideon and you don't have to feed him all the time."

"Mark didn't eat with us all the time," Esther piped up to say.

"*Neh*," her mother agreed, looking regretful, "and we miss him being here. He played with the *Kinder* and helped out cheerfully whenever he was needed."

"Have you heard whether he arrived in Windber yet?" Sarah carefully spoke in a casual voice. There was no reason to act as if she had special interest in the *Mann*, after all.

Looking to her daughter for confirmation, Hagar said, "I believe Gideon did just say he'd gotten a letter from Josiah."

"*Yah*, *Daed* did get one." Esther was very certain.

Sarah got the impression that this child was usually certain. Since she'd observed Esther's younger sister speak with the same confidence, Sarah could only guess this was a *familye* trait. Hopefully, James knew how to stand his ground.

"That's right." Hagar clearly remembered now. "Josiah mentioned—when giving Gideon family news—that Mark was being very helpful on the farm. He understandably thanked us for sending Mark his way."

"How are Leah and Josiah's *familye*?" The words came out readily as friendliness and curiosity both came naturally to Sarah.

"Very *gut*," Hagar said. "All are well, thank *Gott*."

Nodding, Sarah responded, "This is very good news."

With more studied casualness, she added, "Is it a small place? Windber? Lots of families? Lots of *Youngies*?"

Hagar shrugged. "I believe the place is of middling size. They seem to have all they need."

This sounded a tad daunting in that it seemed there would be a good number of *Maedels* around Mark. Well, she thought, he was like a lost puppy with no direction. Any girl willing to court with such a *Mann* wasn't thinking ahead.

"It's to be hoped," she said with what she hoped was seen as kindness, "that Mark chooses a work direction for himself soon. I would think that will affect his finding a *Frau*."

"I am sure," Hagar laughed, "that this was not his purpose in going to Windber. Still, *yah*, a *Mann's* condition in this world always matters in such things as marriage. That and his reliance on *Gott*, but Mark is so *Schmaert*, he has many choices. I'm sure he will soon find work to suit him."

Sarah smiled, the expression requiring effort. It was surely none of her business who Mark married. "Of course, you are right. My *Daed* said the same about him."

CHAPTER SIX

"Bishop Schrock came by the *Haus* several days ago." Jesse spoke heavily.

Visiting in Mannheim before he returned to Windber for another couple of weeks, Mark looked at his *Bruder*. "Go on. Was he just here to welcome you back? Why so glum? We grew up with the Schrock boys and played at the Schrock *Haus*."

"*Yah*, but it wasn't that kind of visit."

Mark waited while Jesse passed a hand over his beard, his expression troubled.

"He spoke to me about remarrying..." The older brother looked up. "Hannah only died a short time ago and I just moved the *Kinder* back home recently."

"Hannah..." Mark started, "she died more than a year ago, Jesse. *Yah*, you only moved home a few months ago and bought the store here, but Hannah's been gone a while now."

While not given to weeping fits and dwelling on his feelings, Mark knew that grief was unique for different people.

"It might be time," he said not unkindly, "to think about giving the *Kinner* a new *Mamm*. You, too, need a *Frau* by your side. This is *Gott's* will. You know you deserve to be happy."

Jesse pressed his lips together before saying, "Hannah and I were very happy. From the time we met when I went to Montegue on my *rumspringa*, I knew I could rely on her, that she would always be by my side."

"I'm sure that—if she could—she would be at your side still." Mark shifted in his seat. It wasn't in his nature to tell others what they should do, but Jesse was his *Bruder* and he was facing a lonely situation.

"Perhaps," his brother conceded in a dismissive voice, "but I'm busy with the store now and just getting settled here back in Mannheim."

"It must be thought of."

"*Yah*, and I will look around me," Jesse said in that same brisk tone. "Not at a young girl, though—"

Mark shifted to relief to speak as casually as his brother. "You grew up here. You've known all these *Maedels* from birth. I would think this would help."

"I'm sure it will—when I get to looking—but time has passed and we are all different people."

"Not all," Mark said, cracking a smile as he thought of Sarah, who'd been spirited since she'd settled in with Enoch and Kate.

"True, but I think I'd want a *Frau* who has seen a little of life. We have some women here now that didn't grow up in Mannheim. Some not as young."

"I suppose so," conceded Mark. "It doesn't really matter, as long as you move forward in life."

"I guess not," Jesse agreed, "but not now. Now I am trying to get this place in shape. The Bontreger's were getting older and missed some things as they ran this store. I'm working things out."

"Well, it's *gut* you have Anna helping with the *Kinner* and Sarah helping here at the store."

"*Yah*," mused Jesse. "I saw Anna playing with the *Kinner* just the other day. They seemed…really happy."

Driving up to his *Haus* late one afternoon after putting in a full day at the store a week later, Jesse frowned to see a black buggy in the drive at the front. He parked, using the water pump at the side of the *Haus* to fill a bucket for the horse. It would have made sense to stable old Topaz now in the shed she occupied at night, but for some reason he felt impelled to go inside right away. The buggy out front didn't belong to Mark or any of Jesse's other *familye*.

If Bishop Schrock had returned, Jesse didn't want to leave Anna dealing with him alone.

He jogged up the front porch steps and opened the screen door just a soft woman's scream echoed from the front room. Stepping inside hurriedly, he saw Anna on the drab green couch there, her hands covering her face as she sobbed. Bishop Schrock and Abraham Zook, older *Mann* in their congregation, stood in front of Anna, their faces heavy.

"I'm sorry, *Frau* Hershberger," the bishop was saying in a solemn tone. "*Gott* knows your pain and those who knew your *Mamm* share this, as well."

"What has happened?" Dread filled Jesse's middle.

"You can't be right," Anna cried. "It can't be her!"

As Anna sat weeping softly into her hands, Bishop Schrock turned to answer in his ponderous way. "*Frau* Lehman's buggy was hit by an *Englischer's* car."

"*Neh!*" Jesse came forward, stepping around the *Menner* to sit next to Anna. "Tell me. Is she injured?"

Even as he asked the question, he realized the Bishop and Abraham wouldn't have come to tell Anna this if her *Mamm* were still alive.

"*Frau* Lehman is dead." Abraham's expression was as somber as his words.

At that moment, Anna's sobs came a little louder, her body shaking so that she lowered a hand as if to steady herself on the couch.

Jesse spontaneously covered her hand with his. Flooded with concern and empathy, he said nothing as he looked at her with understanding. On the seat next to him, Anna's whole body shook with her sobs.

Jesse knew the horror of this kind of news. He also had loved greatly and lost. Anna had no other relatives and had loved her *Mamm* very much.

"You cannot be right." Her words were almost inaudible through her sobs and Jesse's clasp tightened on her hand as it shifted to convulsively return his grip. "I left her only hours ago. She was fine!"

"I'm sorry," the bishop said again. "The *Englischer* car was going very fast."

"From what we heard," Abraham offered, "the police seemed to think the driver was impaired by too much drink."

"Our great condolences," the bishop offered after a moment, seeming not to know what else to say.

Sitting on the couch beside Anna, her small hand in his, Jesse heard the kitchen door slam and turned to see both Joel and Levi peering around the kitchen door, their faces wide-eyed and serious.

"You will be okay," Jesse uttered mechanically, hating that he could now only think of words that hadn't comforted him in his time of anguish.

"She is gone! She is gone. *Mamm*! Oh, *Mamm*!"

Anna's hopeless cry echoed so much of the pain he'd known himself. Jesse used his other hand to beckon his sons forward. They also knew the ache of grief and they loved Anna. She'd been like a *Mamm* to them.

At his gesture, Levi rushed forward, followed more slowly by his older *Bruder*, Joel. Levi clutched at Anna's skirt, his sobs almost as loud as hers. Standing next to where she sat, Joel patted her shoulder awkwardly.

"You have us, Anna," he offered. "You always have us."

Feeling a small swell of happiness amidst all this pain, Jesse was glad his sons had kindness for another. If he'd had to guess, he'd have thought the slam of the kitchen door was his poor little Evie, running out to the comfort of the chickens or goats. She'd done just the same when his poor Hannah had died.

"I just don't…" Anna gasped for air. "I just don't know what I'll do!"

"Pray for *Gott* to give you comfort, my *Dochder*. Pray."

Jesse knew this was a good recommendation, but it probably sounded inadequate in the face of her suffering. His hand still covering Anna's, he bent his head, these silent words rising to his Lord's ears.

"Please help her, Gott, and please, please help me know how I can ease her grief."

Later that afternoon, Sarah rushed into their *Haus*. *"Mamm! Mamm!"*

From her seat in the kitchen, Kate looked up from the butter she was churning.

Swallowing convulsively, Sarah sat on a stool she scooted close to her *Mamm's* side.

Kate lifted her brows in question, continuing to rhythmically churn the butter. She asked with a gentle smile, "What's upset you, *Dochder?*"

Sarah swiped at her damp eyes. "It's Anna. Her *Mamm* was in a terrible buggy accident this morning. An *Englischer* hit her with his car and…and her *Mamm* is dead!"

Kate released her grip on the churn dasher allowing it to sink into the crock. "No? Leah? No!"

Sarah swallowed again, nodding as her eyes filled with tears. She'd grown up knowing the dangers of *Englischers'* fast-moving cars.

Reaching out, her *Mamm* squeezed her knee comfortingly. "This is terrible news. Anna only had her *Mamm*, after that the *Schlang* she married abandoned her! She doesn't even have *Kinder.*"

Kate shook her head sorrowfully.

"Neh," responded Sarah. "I always thought that might be best since he left and then got killed, but now Anna has no one! No one, but her friends and neighbors."

Her cheeks wet with the tears now leaking out of her eyes, Sarah nodded. "It is all so unfair!"

"Now, as you know, *Dochder,"* Kate began again rhythmically lifting the churn paddle, "that life in this world isn't fair, sweet girl. *Gott* has told us that this world is not our home, but Anna isn't alone. She blessed to have friends and relatives. We will take her in and do all we can, you know."

"*Yah*," Sarah responded darkly, "but this is not the same as having a home and a husband on which you can rely."

Her mother looked over at her. "Of course, not, but we cannot understand *Gott's* works."

"Yes, this is true." Sarah brooded on the situation. There was no question that *Gott* watched over all who let Him. "Still, life on this earth is uncertain and...and sometimes frightening."

"It can certainly be so. This is why we must remember there is life beyond this world and we must know that things sometimes are worked out in better ways than we could have planned."

Glancing at Kate with a compassionate look, Sarah said, "I know how blessed you are to be married to the *Mann* you've always loved."

Her *Mamm* frowned. "You must not think that I—or *Gott*—wished your own father dead! *Gott* never kills or hurts. He is only love."

"Of course, and we couldn't have found a better place than with *Daed*." Sarah gazed across the living room unseeing, "Still, you went to Enoch back then. You asked him to marry you and take us in. You took action to keep from marrying Aaron, the Bishop's *Youngie* son. Aren't we told that *Gott* has given us minds to use? We must do our part. We must choose the best lives we can in this world. Isn't that what it means to live a godly life?"

"I suppose." Her mother had stopped churning, looking at Sarah with concerned eyes.

"There is no denying that this is a frightening, uncertain world," Sarah said in a voice that sounded hard to her own ears. "Anna's husband left her. Left this life...and now her mother is dead."

She knew this was more indication for her to find a settled, reliable father for her own *Kinder*. She must marry a *Mann* on whom she could rely.

"*Goedemorgen*," Sarah said as she came into the store the next morning. "You're here in Mannheim again!"

Mark looked up from shifting the shelves he'd made for the store, a little annoyed with himself that his pulse had sped up. "*Yah*, I finished working with Josiah."

"For good?"

"Yes," he shifted the shelf into its resting spot.

"You didn't find your place in Windber, either?"

"*Neh.*" Mark's mouth kicked up on one side. It seemed he and Sarah had picked right back up where they'd left off.

"This doesn't surprise me," she said.

"Are you courting now with any of the *Menner* here?" He couldn't resist asking.

"Wouldn't you like to know," Sarah returned smartly. "Our Sings are full of promising young men."

"This is *gut* for you," he retorted, not yet able to wipe the grin off his face.

"Are you any closer to finding a job you want to keep?" she shot back. "Now that you've left Josiah and Leah's farm."

Mark started laughing, shaking his head. "I've missed you, Sarah."

"I can't imagine why." She looked back at the office behind the register, Jesse having made a sound inside.

"Oh, Jesse is here already. I guess Anna must have gone in to watch his *Kinder*. I thought she might stay away a day longer."

"I heard about Anna's loss," Mark said somberly. "Jesse told us last night. Is she okay?"

Concern darkened Sarah's expressive face as she shook her head. "It's *baremlich*, just terrible. She is staying with us now. I didn't know she'd left our *Haus* to go to Jesse's. The girl's grief is so strong."

"Of course." He nodded. "To have gone off to work one day and then her *Mamm* is *poof*! just gone! How could she not be distressed. I guess being with Joel, Levi and Eve will help her with her grief, though."

Sarah came slowly to stand by the shelf he'd just finished. "I don't know. I was very young when my *Daed* died—and I had Kate. She was and is wonderful. Anna doesn't have anyone besides us. I don't think I grieved as much as Anna is."

He made a protesting sound in his throat. "You cannot compare the two. As you said, you were small and you had a *Mamm*. You couldn't have known what was happening. Small *Kinder* don't understand death."

Pausing for a moment, Mark said reflectively, "I'm not sure I do. It's out of knowing our grief and confusion at loss that *Gott* said this first death is like a sleep. Although this frightens some. Sleep is such a *gut* thing, in our minds. We are told, though, that there will be another life, another world. Anna will see her *Mamm* again."

"That is true," Sarah responded tartly, "but that doesn't change her pain now."

"*Neh*," he agreed. "Jesse is very concerned about her. He said this several times. No one could understand loss more than he."

"Of course." Sarah glanced toward the store's office. "Naturally, he would, having had his *Frau* and his children's *Mamm* die."

Mark felt her gaze rest on his face for a thoughtful moment. "It must be very difficult for him to be alone... To be single with what, Anna says, are three energetic *Kinder*."

A smile spreading across his face at the thought of his *Niblings*, Mark agreed, "Joel, Levi and Eve are definitely energetic. Fun, too. I hope to have *Kinder* half so lively."

"Is he...?"

Sarah had such an expression of studied casualness that the grin faded from his face and Mark immediately grew suspicious. The girl's expression was so open, her thoughts could almost be said to be printed there.

"Do you know if he's...looking to marry again soon?" She glanced at him. "It would be normal, of course."

A terrible possibility sudden dawned in Mark's head and he swiveled his head to look at her fully. She couldn't be thinking...

Even as he thought it, Mark knew Sarah could be seriously considering Jesse as a possible husband. She'd said she wanted someone who would always provide and not leave his *familye* in want as her father had done, but Jesse, for all his good qualities, wasn't the *Mann* to handle Sarah.

"*Neh.* You're not the *Maedel* for Jesse," Mark said flatly.

"What?" she bridled, indignation on her vivid face.

"You don't need to consider yourself as Jesse's next *Frau.*"

"What do you know about anything?" she retorted. "You aren't the one who gets to decide what others do."

It swiftly occurred to Mark that Sarah could be contrary, doing just what she was told she shouldn't do. He absolutely didn't want to encourage the *Maedel* in this direction. Gritting his teeth to hold back an outpouring of speech, Mark took a deep breath. Without a doubt, he knew Sarah wasn't the woman for his brother. Why he knew this with such certainty, he couldn't say, but he was very sure.

"*Neh,* I'm not in charge of this. We don't mind the business of others, though," he responded automatically.

"No!" Sarah looked at him with indignation, tossing her head.

It was strange, but her spirited response evoked in him a bizarre desire to draw her into his arms and kiss her senseless. Of course, he didn't do it.

"I just meant," Mark said, holding himself on a tight rein, "that Jesse is busy getting his business going and hasn't talked of finding another *Frau.*"

Maybe he'd said that in too sharp a tone, he realized, but she absolutely needed to rethink her plan.

Sarah stared at him, suspiciously. "You don't need to snarl at me."

"I'm not snarling." His response would have been more convincing if he hadn't made it so short.

"You are, too," she responded in a cooler voice. "What are you so upset about? It's not like I'm saying *you* should marry."

"*Neh*," he snapped, "because a *Maedel* would be crazy to marry a *Mann* who hasn't a store or who at least a farm."

"Good grief," she said, "calm down. We're not talking about you."

Mark bit back words that crowded onto his tongue. His ire about this was stupid, he told himself, trying to settle into his usual tone.

"I was referring to your *Bruder*," she said, readjusting a can on the shelf.

A red flash went over Mark again and faded away as he began to realize what had made him so angry. He liked Sarah and didn't want her to embarrass herself. That was all this was.

"Jesse will take another *Frau*," he said, level now, "but I imagine she will be a widow with *Kinder* of her own."

"Maybe," Sarah responded, "but if this loss of Anna's tells us anything, it shows that life can be short and can be very sad. Jesse lost the mother of his children and now Anna has lost her beloved *Mamm*."

"This is true."

"We...must remember this." Her face was serious. "Anna has no *Mann* now, since that faithless Hiram Hershberger left her and the church. How can a girl not want to marry a *Mann* who will do everything to keep his *Frau* and his *Kinder* safe, should he not be in this world?"

Saying nothing, Mark looked at her.

"*Gott* has given us guidance. He tells us He loves us and wants us to be loving toward others as well as ourselves. I think that means He wants *Maedels* to make sure they rely on the best in this life."

Mark reflected a moment on what she'd said. Sarah still wasn't the right woman for Jesse—of that he was convinced—and yet he couldn't completely argue with her logic. "*Yah*, that is true, but this cannot be a *Maedel's* only concern. She must love her *Mann*."

"Of course," Sarah said with a dismissive wave of her hand that left a niggling uneasiness in his stomach. "That goes without saying."

Later that evening, Mark slouched into the bedroom Grace shared with their younger sisters, Claudia & Amity. Only Grace was there in the rocker by the window, her lap full of blue material as she hemmed the wide skirt.

She smiled up as he sat on her bed.

"*Hallo*, Twin."

"*Hallo*."

He could feel her studying him, knowing questions would be quick to follow.

"What?"

"Nothing," she said, looking back at the fabric in her lap.

"Go ahead," he said, "I can tell when you have something to say."

She chuckled before admitting, "It does seem to me that something is bothering you."

"Not really." He traced an invisible design on the bedspread while she said nothing, seeming to wait for him to speak.

"I had another talk with Sarah."

Grace gave him a questioning look. "She works for our *Bruder* in the store. As you were there helping him today, I would have thought you'd run into Sarah."

"*Yah*, but we always seem to end up at the same spot."

Some niggle nudged him to tell Grace about Sarah's accusations.

"Your work?"

"Always." He fell back to lie on her bed. "She speaks as if I shove myself into whatever job I come to."

"I don't think she means that." Grace wrinkled her nose. "You said she's fun and easy to talk to."

"She is, except when she talks about my work, which is more and more the case."

"You have to admit her concerns are natural. Most *Maedels* want a husband who will care for the *familye*."

"I don't even have a *familye*," he complained.

"And you won't have one until you find what *Gott* has intended for you?"

"No, I won't and it doesn't matter how much Sarah pushes me about this."

"You know," his twin said in a dispassionate voice. "You really are stubborn as a mule."

Mark's laughter rang out. "Yes, I guess I am."

His sister shook out the dress skirt in her lap. "You must be careful, *Bruder*."

"What do you mean?"

"Don't cut off your nose to spite your face."

"I don't see that I'm doing that," he objected.

"Of course, you don't," Grace said in a resigned voice. "Think what you want, Mark. Decide what you really want…and then ask yourself if Sarah's wish is out of line."

CHAPTER SEVEN

Dear Gott, Sarah prayed that evening, *I know you are with Anna in her grief. I know that you will guide her as to what is best right now. Help me to be with her, to comfort her, in spite of my own grief.*

Tears leaked through Sarah's closed eyes.

I know that you led Mamm and me to Enoch and I ask that you now lead me to make the best choices. Help me know what these are, Gott. I don't think I could be as strong as Kate. She took a child that wasn't even her own—she took me, Gott—and struggled terribly after my Daed-Jakob died. I pray that you guide me, Gott. That you help me choose a husband—a partner—on whom I can rely.

Help me, Gott.

"I always like you finding the time to visit me out here," Isaac bent to kiss Mercy, his *Frau.*

A few days after Anna's loss, the two were in Isaac's woodshop with Mark working on one of Isaac's several projects that were stacked around the shed.

"You should be appreciative," Mercy responded to her husband with a smile. "I have many chores to do in the *Haus.*"

"Do you two mind?" Mark asked in a long-suffering voice. "All this smooching and sweetness is making me *grank*."

Isaac laughed, not noticeably offended. "I'm sorry seeing us makes you sick, but, if marital happiness upsets you, you probably shouldn't work here."

"I guess not," Mark agreed.

"*Mamm*!" A *Buwe* of six or seven stuck his head around the door. "Rachel's gotten into the goat pen again!"

"*Denki*, Aaron! You're a *gut* boy for watching after her." She nuzzled her husband's cheek. "I must go get that naughty *Bobbli*."

"At least she didn't sneak in the hen house this time," Isaac called after her with a grin. "That little girl has the greatest attraction to animals."

"And they seem to sense that she means them no harm," Mark added. He'd only worked with Isaac a few days, but he knew Mercy's youngest—only a small child of two or three years—had gained the reputation in her short life of being loved by goats and chickens alike.

Isaac and his brothers all seemed to have happy homes. Mark knew this wasn't always the case.

He looked down at the piece of wood he was sanding, seeing instead Sarah's face when she'd stated her determination to marry a *Mann* who'd never let his *familye* down. Like her father had.

Was he like that? Mark rubbed the sandpaper with the woodgrain as Isaac had taught him. *Yah*, he liked moving around, trying out different jobs in different places, but did that make him unreliable?

Drawing in a deep breath, he irritably reminded himself that—unlike Sarah's *Daed*—he had no one dependent on him. It made no difference if he stayed in one job or owned a farm.

"Was it hard to decide to do this work?" he asked Isaac.

His employer looked up at Mark's sudden question. After a moment, he said, "*Yah*. Yes, it was. As you may know, I own the farm here. When I was younger, I worked the land, but made furniture when I could."

"You farmed?"

"I did," Isaac said, nodding. "With my *Eldre's* help, I bought this land. I knew farming. I'd grown up with that life and we just built whatever we needed. If we required a bed, we made a bed."

Mark nodded. This was how many people managed, building what they needed, some sturdier and better than others.

"The building of furniture became more and more interesting, though, as I got older. More satisfying. Doesn't *Gott* direct us to do the work we do best? I—I ended up seeing that I was better at this. More fit for this than for farming."

Blowing sawdust off the wood in front of him, Mark said with a rueful grin, "I guess I'm not sure what I'm best fitted for."

At that moment, Mercy popped her head around the workshop door, asking in an exasperated voice, "Has Rachel come through here?"

"I'll find her," the child's mother said in a determined voice before she disappeared from the doorway.

"This little girl is a handful, certainly more than her *Geschwischder* ever were."

"You have a nice *familye*," Mark said abruptly.

Isaac's smile widened. "I do. *Yah*."

"I want a *familye* one day myself."

His boss looked at him. "*Yah*. You can arrange that, I'm sure."

Clenching his mouth shut, Mark decided that, in his current mood, he should say no more.

The next week passed in a blur for Sarah. Between comforting a grieving Anna, who still stayed with them on the farm, Sarah also handled her chores and worked at the store. Although she'd had *Menner* display interest in her for several years now, Sarah wasn't sure the best way to ingratiate herself to Jesse, now that she'd begun to see him as a possible husband.

She smiled when she saw him at work—although surely she'd done this before—and displayed interest in his *Kinder*, but she wasn't sure how to move things into a more personal interaction.

Working alongside him and hearing from Anna about Joel, Levi and little Eve only took her so far. It felt awkward, trying to introduce this new romantic note into their interactions, but Sarah was determined.

She wasn't going to end up like Anna, like when Kate was after her *Daed*-Jakob died.

Having checked out *Frau* Glick's purchases at the counter, Sarah returned to put back on the shelves several items that had been decided against by various customers.

"Hey! Jesse! Sarah! Come help!"

Looking up at the call, she glanced toward the back of the store.

Running through the store, she burst open the back door to find Mark bearing a sturdy armchair, all simple and clean.

"Hey! Hold the door open while I bring this in!"

"Why are you bringing it into the store?" She stepped back to give him room to pass.

Mark grinned. "Jesse had Isaac make a strong chair for the front of the store, so customers could rest there."

"That's nice," she commented as he carried in the chair. "Jesse is nice that way."

Sarah followed him as he walked through the store, noticing the easy way he balanced what had to be a weighty piece of furniture, his back straight and his arm muscles bulging.

Looking away, she chastised herself, refusing to even let herself think about this.

Mark sat the chair by a window at the front of the store, shifting it to face the register. "There. Jesse can move it, if he wants."

"Yes." Still battling with thoughts she knew were wrong, she said no more.

"My *Bruder* is a nice *Mann*," Mark said abruptly, "but he's a *Mann*, just the same."

"*Yah*," she said, as confused by his words as by his uncharacteristic sternness.

"He's not the *Mann* for you, though. Definitely not."

Affronted by Mark's statement, she demanded, "Why ever not? Never mind! Is this your decision? No! I thought we settled this. We have no business sticking our noses into other people's business and you have nothing to say about who marries who!"

He said nothing for a moment, his face stern, the clenching of his jaw visible.

"I just mean that Jesse's not the *Mann* for you," Mark said in a stubborn voice, "and you need to move on. He's been through a lot. He's not perfect, as none of us are, but he will find his way when this is right."

Irritated, Sarah braced her hand on her hip. "What is it with you? Do you think Jesse needs a keeper?"

"*Neh*," he shot back, "but you might!"

She felt her face prickle with an angry flush. "Let me tell you this, Mark Fisher! Who I marry or what I do is no concern of yours!"

He just looked at her with an unimpressed expression.

"Do you hear?" she demanded, stalking over to where he stood by the chair. "I am just as *gut* as any other *Maedel* and your *Bruder* would be lucky to get me!"

Seeming unmoved, Mark responded curtly, "I never said you weren't as *gut* as other *Maedels*, just that Jesse isn't the *Mann* for you."

"You," she stabbed her finger into his broad chest, her breath quickened by her anger, "don't get to decide that, do you?"

He looked down at her, his face all tense. "I don't understand why you don't value yourself more. Don't you think you deserve to find a *Mann* who fits with you?"

"I think," she uttered with fury, "that I am determined not to end up married to a *Mann* who doesn't protect me or our *Kinner*. I deserve a *Mann* who won't leave me—should he die—as my father left Kate, penniless and with a child to support. Not even her own child, either! I deserve better than that and I'm determined not to marry a *Mann* who can't settle into one kind of work. One who flits around from job to job, with no thought of building for his— or his *familye's*—future! I know Isaac Miller asked you to work with him, to settle into the furniture building business, but you said no!"

They stood facing one another, Sarah's chest heaving with her rage and distress and Mark looking like he was carved of stone.

"I was a little girl, Mark." She fought to keep her tears at bay. "My *Mamm* faced having either to marry a *Youngie*—barely old enough to shave—or ask the *Mann* who hated her to marry her! Thank God, Enoch loved her as much as he hated her...or I don't know what would have become of us."

"Did your father's people not offer to take in you and Kate?"

His tone seemed to have softened, but she was too far gone to pay much attention.

"*Neh*," she swallowed and tried to steady her words. "My *Daed* was the youngest of his *familye* and his *Geschwischder* didn't live here. They were older, had families of their own and were trying to care for their *Eldre*. They were only too happy to leave me to my *Mamm*—Kate—and to have her assisted by those in Mannheim."

Sarah shook her head. "I'm sure they would have said she should marry Aaron Yoder."

"The Bishop's son? Why he must have been..."

"A *Youngie*, like I said," Sarah turned and sank into the chair Mark had brought in. She felt drained, like a wet rag that had been wrung out.

The heat seemed to have gone out of his words, too. She felt almost too tired to notice.

"I will never be in that position," she said flatly. "I am determined."

"*Yah*," he said slowly. "I can see how that would leave you determined. Do you never have contact with your *Daed*—with Jakob's—people?"

"Of course, I do," she responded, relieved that her voice sounded stronger and more normal. "Every so often, they drive through here and stop to visit."

"*Gut*." He still seemed quiet and thoughtful.

Sarah wished she hadn't been so open, hating her own transparency. She certainly didn't want Mark to pity her.

"And you say that Jesse and the children are doing well? They've been wonderful to Anna. Truly a blessing."

"*Yah*," Mark said. "*Yah*, Anna is a blessing herself."

Looking struck by an idea, she said, "You know, *Menner* need to recognize what a good *Frau* she'd make. She's funny and loyal. A *Mann* could do a lot worse. Anna's a treasure."

Anna needed a *Mann* to love her and a *familye* now more than ever.

"She's very *gut* girl," he responded, looking shook.

Sarah wished she'd guarded her tongue and not spilled out the distress she'd felt when her *Daed* died, but maybe Mark wouldn't just see her as a *Maedel* determined to get herself a well set-up husband.

Maybe now he'd recognize that she had valid reasons behind her ambition... Maybe the fear she'd had when her *Daed* died hadn't been obvious.

"You know, Anna," Sarah told her friend when the two sat together at the church meeting later that week, "you know that you can stay with us as long as you need. There is no rush to settle on a direction."

"You and Kate and Enoch—the whole *familye*—have been wonderful to me," Anna said in her soft voice as the two of them sat to the rear of the room. Around them bustled several *Frau*, shepherding their *Kinder* to the kitchen to get the after-meeting lunch meal.

"I think my biggest worry," she continued, "is that I see no direction. I could take a job helping old *Frau* Stoltfus at her bed and breakfast out on the highway, I suppose. *Englischers* often stop there for a night or two of living in our way. She often needs help and hires different girls to do her heavy work."

"You could do that." Sarah tried not to look doubtful, returning the smile of a passing *Mann* with whom she and Anna went to school. "I'm sure it would be a very *gut* job."

"Yes, and it might start to feel like a *familye* eventually."

Anna's quiet words made Sarah want to cry. Forgetting all about the smiling *Mann* who'd passed by, she wondered if she should mention the marriage possibility to Anna again. What she'd said the other day was true. Anna would make someone a good wife.

Although she'd thought of Mark marrying her friend, the thought didn't settle comfortably in her head. Besides, he'd himself had said he wasn't ready for a wife...or something like that.

"Jesse has been kind. I don't know what I'd do without Joel and Levi and Eve to care for." Anna turned suddenly to her friend. "I was surprised, as I told your *Eldre*, that the insurance people from the *Englischer* who hit *Mamm* came to see me. We were all startled when they came to the *Haus*."

Sarah turned in her chair. "*Yah*, I was just leaving for my job when they came. So surprising to see *Englischers* there. I forgot to ask what they said when I got home. Anything important?"

"I don't know. There was something about a money settlement for the *Englischer* having killed *Mamm* in that accident." Anna shook her head, her eyes filling with tears. "I didn't follow it all. Apparently, something's still being settled. They asked if I had a lawyer."

A different young *Mann* appeared in front of them, smiling. "*Hallo, Frau* Hershberger. Remember me? Bart Zook? I believe we were in school together."

Anna quickly masked the surprise look on her face. "*Yah*, I do remember. *Hallo*."

"I hope you're coming to the Sing at our *Haus* this evening." Bart Zook looked over his shoulder, "Oh, the food must be coming from the kitchen. My *Mamm* is motioning to me. Goodbye!"

The two girls watched him disappear into the crowd.

"Well, that's interesting," Sarah said, scorn dripping from her words. "He acts as if he hasn't seen you all this time."

"I know," Anna agreed in an astonished tone. "Whatever has come over Bart?"

She glanced at Sarah. "Why he's never paid me the least attention and his *Mamm—Frau* Zook—has been downright frosty since Hiram left. I always thought she blamed me."

"As if you made him leave you and the church," Sarah agreed staunchly. "*Gott* has given us all the power over our own lives."

Anna seemed dazed. "I don't think I was ever particularly invited to a Sing at the Zook *Haus*, not even before I married."

Knitting her brow, Sarah said slowly, "Enoch came to the store today to buy some things for the farm. He had some other errands, too."

She looked at her friend. "Do you think he told anyone about the insurance people coming to see you?"

"He may have. It was certainly no secret."

"And he'd know that many are worried about your future. He might have mentioned the possible settlement." She scowled into the crowd where Bart Zook at stood. "Some *Menner* are such pigs. Pigs are better!"

"Why should Enoch not have spoken of the insurance people?" Anna looked confused.

"I wasn't calling Enoch a pig. Bart!"

"Oh." Anna still looked confused.

Sarah spelled out her suspicion. "Have you noticed *Menner* paying more attention to you? After the news of you getting money from that insurance settlement? *Gott* has said that we humans are weak and this is very much so!"

"*Neh!*" Anna stared at the church members around them. "Surely this isn't so! Our friends can't be motivated by money this way."

"Yes, they can," Sarah snapped. "Has Bart Zook or any other *Menner* smiled at you so particularly since Hiram left?"

"Not really." Anna seemed to dim.

"It was almost as if you disappeared to all eligible *Menner*, until now. *Schlangs!*"

"Financial responsibility is important," Anna offered sadly. "And I don't suppose the insurance money to be a big amount."

"Of course, but you are worthy. You always were, despite Hiram's actions."

"What you say is true," her friend said, looking even more despondent. "If the possibility on a settlement makes people this different, it is very difficult to know who to trust."

"*Yah*." Sarah started tapping her chin, a new thought having occurred to her. This new possibility made a marriage for Anna even more likely. She'd always wanted a *familye* of her own. Hadn't Sarah herself been thinking that marriage would help Anna deal with her grief?

"This might be…a *gut* thing, Anna," she said.

"*Gut*?" her friend turned a startled gaze toward Sarah. "To think our friends may have such a motivation for marriage?"

"*Neh*, not that, but this makes them really look at you. See you as more than that *Schlang's* abandoned wife," Sarah responded in a brisk voice.

"Oh." Anna fell silent.

"Don't you see, my friend? You could have *Kinder* of your own. A *familye* like you always wanted. Yes," Sarah went on, "you will always love and mourn your *Mamm*, but you wouldn't be alone."

Anna reached over to pat her hand. "I will always be grateful that your *familye* has been kind to me."

Sarah smiled. "Don't you know? You're a part of our *familye*. I believe everyone in our church loves you—they just haven't always seen you—"

With a brave smile, Anna stuck in "*Eldre* fear their *Kinner* doing as Hiram did. I am a reminder of that."

"His action had nothing to do with you," Sarah dismissed. "Maybe they'll come to see that now."

The summer sun being high in the sky later that week, Jesse rested in the *Haus* shadow before heading back to work on cleaning out the barn. In his hand, he held a glass of cool water from the pump.

Bumble bees hummed in flowering bushes at the corner of the porch, and all seemed peaceful. *Gott's* world looked beautiful and calm around him. He could hear Joel and Levi chattering a few yards away with Anna in the garden behind the *Haus*.

Smiling at their cheerful voices, he registered that little Eve was playing in a dirt pile nearby.

He was glad that, despite her grief, Anna felt comfortable here with the children. His mouth pulling down, he reflected that he could understand some of what she must feel, having lost her mother.

"...and we had chickens on the farm," young Levi's voice filtered up to him from where the *Buwe* sat in between garden rows.

"Chickens are friendly," Anna commented. "A *Mann* in our church even had a chicken who would ask for hugs."

"Not a boy chicken, I'll bet," his son responded wisely. "Roosters just walk around crowing and acting all proud of themselves."

"Not that you ever tried to hug a rooster," Joel scoffed.

"I found a worm in the dirt," Eve called out.

A small smile curved Jesse's mouth as he saw Anna look toward the girl. "What kind of worm, Eve?"

He could see his little *Dochder* hold up a grubby hand.

"This kind that lives in the dirt."

"Ahhh, then put it back, *Liebling*," Anna responded in her soft voice. "I'm sure it was surprised when you found it."

"Anna," his elder son said in a serious voice, "I heard that your *Mamm* died last week."

Jesse felt himself cringe, gripped by a sudden urge to rush in and change what could only be an awkward subject.

"Yes, she did, Joel," Anna responded before he could act, her words sorrowful, but not offended.

For what seemed like a long moment, the summer breeze blew through the grasses around the *Haus* and Jesse felt like he was holding his breath.

"I'm very sad," Anna said eventually. "I miss my *Mamm* so much."

"I miss my *Mamm*," Levi said in his small boy voice, re-entering the conversation.

From his spot in the shadows, Jesse saw her reach over, lift his son's hat and kiss the crown of the boy's head.

She replaced his hat, going wordlessly back to weeding the garden.

"I miss her, too," Joel said in a gruff tone. "I miss her all the time."

Anna stopped. "I bet you do."

Eve, who must have heard the conversation, sat down on the garden furrow nearest Joel's knee. "I cried a lot then. I still cry."

"You cry about everything," Levi said, disgusted.

"Don't be mean to her," Joel inserted. "We all cry sometimes. Even *Daed* did for a while."

Jesse felt himself go still. He'd known his children were watching him after Hannah died, taking their cues from him. He'd tried to soldier on, but he might have known they'd sensed and shared his grief. His wife had been gone a while now, though, and he was gradually beginning to feel alive again.

Enough so to notice Anna, damn him.

And here she was grieving for her mother. He should be ashamed of himself.

"I think," Anna's soft voice came to him from the garden, so close he could almost feel her. "I think we will always miss our mothers. And love them always."

He saw her brush a hand over Joel's thin shoulder.

"But someday your *Daed* will bring home to you another *Mamm*, someone who will love him and you."

"I don't want another *Mamm*," Joel said impatiently.

"No, but you will need someone who loves you, and your *Daed* will, too."

"Maybe, but I won't like her."

At the thought of this potential woman, everything in Jesse felt as mulish as Joel sounded.

"Whoever *Daed* marries," Joel continued. "She won't be like you. She could be bossy and mean."

Anna laughed, her soft chuckle bringing up the hairs on Jesse's neck. "She'll probably be nice, Joel. Your *Daed's* not likely to want to marry a woman who is mean to you."

Jesse saw his son hunch an unconvinced shoulder, thinking he couldn't imagine some other, unknown woman. He wanted a wife who was kind. Soft and sweet…like Anna.

How could he possibly be thinking such things at this moment? Something was seriously wrong with him.

CHAPTER EIGHT

Mark was in the middle of rearranging planks of wood in Isaac's shop two weeks later when Sarah burst around the corner.

"Is it true?" she demanded, her cheeks flushed pink.

"*Goedemorgen* to you," Mark said as innocently as he could, opening his eyes wide. "I hope your morning is *gut*."

He loved how she looked when all ruffled and annoyed. He wouldn't do it, but it made him want to kiss her

"You *Bisskatz*!"

"How am I a skunk?" he asked, the grin fading from his face.

"Did Isaac invite you to go into his business here? Did he?"

Pausing with a rough plank in his hand, he responded shortly, "*Yah.*"

He was getting tired of this conversational topic.

"And you turned him down?"

She seemed incensed by this, Mark noted, annoyed by the intensity she radiated.

"I did." He leaned the plank where he'd been placing the others.

"He has a *gut* business here!"

Knowing he was acting like a jerk, Mark gave her a hard smile. "He does."

Sarah jammed her hands on her hips. "And now you're moving to another job? Mercy said something about you working for Daniel Stoltfus in Elizabethtown? When will this stop?"

Mark exhaled before responding.

"I really don't know, Sarah. Daniel and I haven't discussed how long he'll need me." His answer was simple-minded, he knew, but her attitude about this was starting to annoy him.

"That's not what I meant," she snapped. "What is wrong with you? How could you not accept his offer? This is pleasant enough work here. Isaac is a nice *Mann*. His work is steady."

"Maybe I want something more than 'steady'.

"That is so selfish of you!"

Now as angry as she was, he looked at her with his mouth set in a line.

"Because you'll miss seeing me when I work with Daniel? I'll visit here all the time," Mark reassured her, snidely. "Elizabethtown is close."

"I'm not worried about that!" she denied hotly.

He turned back to the wood he'd been straightening, positioning another plank near the others. "What are you worried about, then? I'm not sure I understand. How is what I do any business of yours?"

Looking over his shoulder at her, his words came out with a crisp edge.

Sarah stood looking at him, saying nothing to this, her eyes growing damp and her mouth wobbly before she finally whirled around and ran out of the shop.

His hand still on the plank, Mark stood unmoving, staring after her as she disappeared through the shop door.

Looking blankly for several minutes at the empty doorway, he swallowed. As much as he teased her and laughed, he realized he hated Sarah being angry with him.

Mark drew in a deep breath, his chest tight as he pushed against a wave of regret. He should probably go after her. Apologize...for something.

Not sure, he argued with himself. Shouldn't she apologize? He couldn't say what he'd done wrong, but—but he knew he hated this.

Leaning the last plank against the wall where Isaac had told him, he took another long breath and then left the shop.

He found Sarah sitting on Isaac and Mercy's wide front porch. She was taking deep gulps of air, apparently trying to calm herself.

He felt like a heel. Swallowing hard, Mark offered quietly, "I'm sorry."

She whirled around at the sound of his voice.

"I'm sorry. I didn't mean to upset you," Mark said, leaning against the porch railing. She hadn't appeared to even notice when he stepped onto the porch.

He felt another pang in his chest, seeing Sarah quickly and hurriedly wipe away a tear that had coasted down her cheek.

"I don't know what you mean," she said in a defensive voice, turning away as she wiped her face.

This wouldn't do. Seeing spunky, lively Sarah like this made him hurt inside.

"It occurs to me," he said, lowering himself to sit on the top porch step at her feet, "that I don't know much about your *Daed*— not Enoch—but your first *Daed*. Will you tell me about him? How old were you when he died?"

She looked at him, her expression deeply suspicious of his grave question. Although before he'd found it easiest to turn any serious moment into a laugh, he couldn't do that now. His return gaze was level.

"Won't you tell me?"

She cast him a wary, doubtful look before saying, "I was eight. Just turned eight, actually."

"And Kate was your *Mamm*?"

"Miriam, the *Mamm* who birthed me, died when I was only a *Boppli*," she answered, her voice calmer now.

Mark turned to look at her, adjusting on the porch railing. "You don't remember her then?"

Shaking her head, Sarah said, "Not really. I just remember Kate. I think I was five or so when she married Jakob, my father."

He felt a smile coast over his face. He liked that she seemed to be easier in talking to him. If about tore him up to have her cry.

This was the most serious conversation they'd ever had and, oddly, it felt very...comfortable. This fragile thread between them felt shaky and new and he found he didn't want to chance disrupting it.

Mark looked out over the Miller's yard, saying in a tone he recognized as different from his usual, "You were young when you were orphaned."

Looking at him, Sarah responded seriously, "*Yah.*"

He exhaled, a short, self-mocking breath. "I didn't recognize it, but I was fortunate, by any standard. I was a troublesome, irritating *Buwe*, when I was younger, always getting into spots where I wasn't supposed to be. I even stayed with my *Grossdaddi* for a short while because of it. I had—have—both a loving *Daed* and *Mamm*. *Geschwischder* and *Grossdaddi* and *Grossmammi*, too. My twin, Grace, and I were blessed from the start."

Saying nothing to this, Sarah looked perplexed. "I'm having difficulty imaging you this way. I mean, I can see you as an annoying kid and I have no difficulty seeing you as a pain."

His laugh was short before he said briefly. "It's true. I was a pain."

Minutes ticked by after he fell silent, the wind shifting through the tops of the trees in the Miller yard as the air between the two of them thickened and seemed to grow warm.

He heard her take a long, anxious breath and he found he didn't want to…upset things between them.

Jumping up after a moment, Sarah blurted out, "I must be going. I'm sure my *Mamm* is wondering why I haven't come back inside. We only drove to Elizabethtown on an errand."

"Sarah—" Mark sat on the edge of the porch, drawing in the dirt beside the steps with a branch he'd found there.

She stared at him, seeming to wait for him to continue.

"I don't know—tell me what that was like—being so young when your *Mamm* died?" He looked up at her then, suddenly wondering how life had been for her young self. "What you remember, anyways."

Her waiting *Mamm* apparently no longer a concern, she abruptly sat back down on the porch bench and said crisply. "I remember it all very well."

Mark looked at her, trying to fathom the uncertainty she'd faced.

"After he died, Kate and I were kicked out of the farm my father rented. We had no *Haus* of our own. No way to earn our living with my father gone."

"What did you do?"

She sat on the bench in front of him, the curve of her cheek soft and sweet.

"I was young, just a *Boppli*," she said, "barely old enough to go to school, but I remember my *Mamm* being cheerfully scared— if you know what I mean. We were living in a *Haus* that was soon to be reclaimed by the farmer who owned it and we had nowhere to go."

It was crazy, the effect this girl had on him and he should probably put as much distance between her and himself as he could, but Mark found he didn't want to. He'd lived his life unfettered, and he'd preferred it that way until he chose to take a wife, which meant he didn't need to seek Sarah out.

A *familye* was a responsibility that he didn't feel ready for…but Sarah tugged at him like no other girl had done.

"I can see why your *Mamm* was scared," he said. "Was there no one amongst your friends to take you in? This is usually the case when one of our own is in trouble. Did you not have *familye?*"

"My *Daed's Geschwischder* weren't in a place where they could take us in." She added with bitterness, "I think they thought she should do as the bishop wished."

"Which was?"

"I told you. Our bishop wanted *Mamm* to marry his son…his barely-out-of-school son."

Mark frowned. "Barely out of school? Your *Mamm* must have been…several years older than him."

"*Yah.* She couldn't bring herself to do it. The only *Mann* she could imagine marrying was Enoch, but they had a complicated history. He wasn't friendly in the beginning. He married her and became my *Daed*, but it was tense, at first." Sarah's expression hardened. "Kate should never have been in that position. It got better with them later, as you must have seen, but I made myself a promise—seeing everything she went through—that I would only entrust myself and my *Kinder* to a *Mann* who wouldn't leave his *familye* to deal with that kind of thing."

Mark shot her a glance, drawing a deep, slow breath.

"I shouldn't—I probably shouldn't have been so open about all this. We are not to complain about our troubles."

"I'm glad you told me," Mark said in a thoughtful voice after a moment, "I can see now why a *Mann's* job matters so much to you. *Yah*, I can see."

He saw alright and he understood in that moment that he was nothing like what she wanted in a *Mann*.

Several days later, Sarah sat next to a sunflower patch with Anna by her side, their long, muted skirts billowing around them on the ground.

Several yards away, rows of maturing sunflowers grew tall with large green flowers topping the stems. Some just showing a fringe of yellow petals, while some had green flower heads with gangly stems, like teen boys, all awkward and slender.

Bright yellow and black bumble bees and their smaller cousins, honey bees, buzzed through the field, mumbling from stalk to stalk. In a few weeks, all the dinner-plate-size centers of the flowers would darken significantly, showing a full ruffle of yellow petals around the edges as the seeds ripened for harvest.

"Don't go into the flower patch too far where I can't see you, Evie," Anna called to the young girl. Turning to Sarah, she commented with a laugh, "I might never find her if she were to lose herself among the sunflowers. Have you ever seen such tall flowers?"

"Only here in Mr. Altorfer's patch," Sarah laughed with her. "His flowers are said to produce many seeds, which bring in a fair amount these days. What fun to bring the *Kinner* here. It'll be like walking through a jungle. So, tell me your news."

Anna flushed, saying "We certainly don't want to trample the crops! I had to promise Mr. Altorfer that we wouldn't break any of the flowers."

"It's a *gut* thing he trusts you! And that the *Kinner* understand farming, but, you said you had something to tell me?"

"*Yah*," she looked self-conscious, "it seems strange and is very unexpected. I can still hardly believe it, but the *Englischers'* insurance company from my mother's buggy wreck came back and brought me a very large check. More settlement money than I ever expected. I could hardly believe it."

"The settlement money!" Sarah was excited for her friend. "Of course, the accident was the *Englischer's* fault—your *Mamm* was always careful when she took out your buggy—but I'd never have expected the *Englischer's* insurance company to own this in any significant way! How wonderful and such a blessing."

"Jesse said the same thing." Anna lowered her voice. "It's thousands of dollars. Several hundred thousand, in fact! I'm sure I don't know what to do."

"I'll bet the *Englischer's* insurance company thought you would have gotten more if you sued them," Sarah said with a dry twist of her lips.

Anna nodded. "Jesse said the same thing."

"You know," Sarah said, excited to find the puzzle pieces falling into place, "I'm sure the *Menner* of this town expected that you'd get some money from the accident, just probably not this much. That's why several particularly talked to you at the service. We wondered, you remember? The insurance people were here to see you before that and several *Menner* definitely treated you differently at our last church meeting."

Her eyes widening, Anna said in a stronger voice, "That must definitely be why they spoke to me that last Sunday! Why they acted like they'd seen me for the first time in years, when I'd seemed invisible before."

"You're now a woman of means," Sarah said, her mouth curving with gleeful laughter. "There's nothing like having a fortune to help others forget your situation. This is a reality. You know what, Anna, this might be the answer to prayers. Maybe now that you are a woman of means, people will start considering you a *gut* match for their sons, like I said. Maybe *Menner* will want to marry you!"

"Oh! I hadn't—" Anna seemed flustered. "—you mean, some *Mann* will want to marry me now that I have money? Some of the *Menner* we have known our whole lives now want to be my husband?"

"I'd definitely think more than one *Mann*," Sarah responded, feeling her eyes dance.

"Well," Anna said after a moment's thought, "I'd like to marry and have a *familye*, but...but it seems wrong to—to profit from my *Mamm's* death. Maybe I shouldn't take this money. I miss her so!"

"You didn't want her death or cause it!" Sarah inserted swiftly. "Maybe this is a blessing from *Gott*, though! A way for you to move past that mess with Hiram."

Anna swallowed, seeming still startled by the thought. "I'd have thought it was a dream, if I didn't have that check and if Jesse hadn't seen the *Englischers* leaving."

Her friend's mention of the *Mann* who Sarah had recently been considering her best husband option gave her pause. If anyone deserved good fortune and blessings, it was Anna. Sarah wouldn't dream of getting in her friend's way.

"I suppose," she said in an offhand voice, "any number of *Menner* will now begin to see all that you offer."

Blinking, Anna said, "I suppose."

"Even more established *Menner*—like Jesse—will probably now consider you a *gut* mate."

Anna glanced at Sarah, seeming to hear in her carefully neutral voice that this might be an issue for Sarah. "Of course not! Not Jesse. He has no interest in me beyond my care for his *Kinder* and he'd not be swayed by the money."

"Don't fail to see the importance of that," Sarah recommended, making the effort to smile. After all, she had other husband choices—maybe not as established as Jesse—but that wouldn't have mattered if he and her friend had developed a closeness. "Your connection with and care for his children is another good reason for Jesse to think of marriage with you."

For some ridiculous reason, Mark's strong image wavered before her mind's eye. She resisted the urge to shake her head. Mark wasn't for her and wasn't even seeking a *Frau*.

Sarah's jaw firmed. She was determined to somehow find a stable husband, even if Jesse was off the market.

Anna ducked her head. "Jesse isn't interested in me, Sarah. There are many others who seek his attention, why he's even noticed you. He told me himself what a *gut* worker you are."

"Well, that's not a ringing commendation," Sarah said, laughing.

She weirdly felt both regret and relief when Anna lifted her head to say with a gentle smile, "*Yah*, it is. *Menner* want a *Frau* who can work hard."

A week later, Mark stopped beside a broad wheelbarrow, putting down the pitchfork. Overhead, the midday sun burned high. As per Daniel's instructions, he was moving hay from a stack to the horse stalls in the barn. The motion of lifting the fork of hay to the wheelbarrow brought a stretch to his muscles.

Sweating in the heat of the day, his shirt clung to his back and he looked around to check whether he was alone. Seeing no one, he pulled the suspenders from his shoulders and unbuttoned the plain shirt his *Schweschders* had made for him.

Flapping his shirt to dry the damp fabric, he stood in the shadow of Daniel and Lydia's barn, wondering what Sarah was doing right then at Jesse's store. A smile curving his mouth, he thought of her light brown hair wisping from under her *Kapp*, her blue eyes snapping with some smart retort he'd made.

His body warmed further as he thought of her, which wasn't his intent.

Sarah was one feisty *Maedel*, that girl. He liked bickering with her, but he hated the two of them being at such odds. Mark was used to making his own choices. *Gott* and the elders offered direction, of course, even his own *Eldre*, but Sarah was none of these. It shouldn't have bothered him that she disapproved of his path.

He shrugged, wriggling his shoulders in attempt to shake loose the nagging feeling. It did matter what she thought, but it shouldn't have.

Just as he thrust his pitchfork again into the pile of hay he was moving, Sarah—of all people—rounded the fence corner by the barn.

"Oh!" she exclaimed, stopping in her tracks at the sight of him.

Startled by the sudden appearance of the girl he'd been thinking about, Mark stared at her for a second.

Suddenly and profoundly aware a moment later of his bare chest and his open shirt, Mark dropped the pitchfork, grabbing to pull his shirt closed. She was here! He hadn't even known Sarah was in Elizabethtown, although it shouldn't have surprised him. Mannheim and Elizabethtown weren't far apart.

"Sarah, you're here," he said in not his most brilliant observation. "I mean, what are you doing here at Daniel and Lydia's?"

Her face startled when she saw him with his open shirt, Sarah had stopped in her tracks and she now looked away pointedly.

"*Hallo*," he offered a standard response while hurriedly buttoning his shirt with awkward fingers, "what are you doing here at Daniel's and Lydia's?"

Her head still averted to closely examine the haystack, she responded, "I'm here with my *Daed* on business related to our buggy. It needs something or other."

"Ahhhhh," he said, his tongue uncharacteristically slow.

"*Whoeeee*? Mark!! Mark!!" An energetic seven-year-old *Buwe* bounced through the open barn door just then, dragging a bicycle-type device behind him.

"I'm here, Jeremiah," Mark responded, knowing the tension between he and Sarah made his words curt.

Not that Daniel and Lydia's oldest seemed affected by this.

"*Hallo*, Sarah!" Jeremiah rushed over to throw his arm around her waist, giving her a big hug, while he held a strange-looking bicycle device to the side.

"*Hallo*, Jeremiah!" She hugged the boy back, her warm smile brightening. "How are you today?"

"I'm *gut*," he said buoyantly. "I'm going to teach Abby how to ride my kick scooter."

"Your scooter?" Sarah looked doubtfully at the bicycle thing. "Isn't your sister too small for that?"

Moving discreetly off to the side as he stuffed his shirttails in his pants' waist, Mark watched the two chat.

"*Neh*," Jeremiah assured her. "Abby is six, just the age my *Daed* bought me my scooter."

"When I saw her gathering eggs just now, she didn't look very big to me," Sarah responded.

"Scooters are easy to ride," Jeremiah proclaimed with all the unfettered confidence of his age. "Aren't they, Mark? There's nothing to it!"

Setting down his kick scooter—a narrow platform suspended low between two bicycle wheels—Jeremiah proceeded to demonstrate this, riding back and forth across the yard, switching his riding and pushing feet back and forth easily.

"I don't know," Mark responded to the *Buwe's* question. "I've always driven buggies or pony carts, even as a scholar."

Jeremiah stopped in his trajectory, looking at Mark with astonishment. "You don't know? You've never ridden a kick scooter?"

Mark laughed at the *Buwe's* surprise. "*Neh*. I never learned to ride one."

"Then you must today," Jeremiah insisted briskly. "Abby won't mind you taking a turn. There she is! Abby, you won't mind Mark taking a scooter lesson, will you?"

"Of course not," the five-year-old girl answered, although it was doubtful she'd heard the entire question, having just joined them by the barn.

"It's her turn," Mark demurred. "Abigail should learn first and you don't need to teach me."

"Go ahead," the sturdy little blonde said, clambering up to sit at the top of the stack of hay he'd been shoveling. "I've been watching Jeremiah ride it a lot and he's already given me one lesson."

Grinning at the matter-of-fact way she said this, Mark bowed toward her small figure.

"*Neh*," Mark said, realizing his desire to avoid looking stupid wasn't making him look any better. Especially since he was being watched by Sarah from not five feet away.

He gestured toward the hay barrow. "Hey, I was directed to move the hay…"

"*Bok, bok, bok*," Sarah mocked softly.

Mark looked her way. "What did you say?"

"*Bok, bok, bok*," she repeated, grinning at him

"I am not a chicken," he responded in a tired voice, glancing her way.

Smirking at him, she flapped her hands at shoulder level.

He had the urge to throttle her and kiss her, at the same time.

Feeling his annoyance rise and determined not to show it, Mark said, "Okay, Jeremiah. Let's have a lesson."

"Great!" Jeremiah danced several side-to-side jigs.

Standing beside him, resigned to looking like a fool, Mark let himself be dragged forward by Jeremiah's grubby hands.

As he was pulled forward, he turned his head so she could hear him, Mark said, "I think Sarah should learn next. Abby won't mind, but before we start my education, are you two sure that your *Mamm* doesn't need you?"

Abigail shook her head vigorously. "*Yah*, we're sure. Andrew and Matthew are napping, as is baby Rachel. The little *Bobbli* is teething, *Mamm* thinks, and *Mamm* was up with her several times."

"Then your *Mamm* deserves this rest," Sarah agreed, climbing up to sit next to the small girl on the haystack. Responding to his dry look by saying. "Stop giving that dirty look, Mark. I have to have a good view. Go ahead and teach him, Jeremiah. Abby and I will watch.

Casting her a rueful smile, he said, "Okay. Show me how your scooter works."

"Okay!" Jeremiah enthusiastically positioned the scooter between the two, the instructor much smaller than his student.

"These are the handlebars, as you can see, and you just need to rest your hands here, on either side."

"Okay..." Mark felt doubtful and shamefully sent up a quick prayer that *Gott* wouldn't let him make a complete fool of himself. *Gott* had never promised he'd always look good, Mark reminded himself, wishing Sarah weren't perched on the haystack with Abby. He could do without her scorn, deciding in that moment to use all his physical prowess to learn to use the scooter.

"See this platform here between the wheels?"

Mark frown attentively at the narrow board suspended between the two wheels. It looked narrow, but he didn't yet have the full details of this device. The scooter wheels were about a foot wide around—smaller than bicycle wheels, but not as small as a man's spread hand. From one end rose a metal pole, to which the handlebars for directing the scooter where attached.

Giving Jeremiah serious attention, Mark tried to block out his awareness of Sarah's form sitting on the haystack to his side.

"You put your hands here," Jeremiah instructed, positioning his hands on either side of the handlebars that surmounted the metal stick part coming up from the wheels.

Mark had seen *Englischer* kids on scooters like this, only with smaller tires than these.

"And you stand here. See? On the flat part between the wheels. No! Don't try to stand on it until you're moving."

"Moving?" Mark knew he wasn't successful at keeping his feeling of stupidity out of his voice. He wasn't used to failing, certainly not within sight of others.

"*Yah*. Of course," Jeremiah responded with excitement. "You're going to run alongside the scooter, jump the flat part with both feet and shoot down the road."

"I'm going to jump on this thing and…shoot down the road?" echoed Mark in as flat a voice as he could. Inside, he could only picture himself jumping onto the flying scooter and falling spectacularly on his face in front of Sarah.

"*Yah!*" Jeremiah continued tootling around on the scooter in the yard next to the Stoltzfus barn.

"Are you sure your *Daed* doesn't need us in the buggy shop?" Mark asked. "We could do this later."

"I'm sure he doesn't need us," Sarah inserted with a big smile. "He's selling my *Daed* a new buggy."

"And he has Able to help him," Jeremiah answered as he scooted past again. "He and Able have handled the buggy shop for years. Able knows a lot more than I do."

"How nice for him."

"Anyway," the small boy said, not noticing that Mark didn't share his enthusiasm, "riding the kick scooter is easy. You'll get it in no time."

"You just have to balance yourself on it," Abigail offered from atop the haystack.

"Balance myself." Mark knew he had decent physical abilities and the kick scooter would probably offer him no real problem. He just didn't want Sarah there to witness his first attempts.

"I bet," he said to Jeremiah, "you and Abby probably took some time to learn this. She's still learning."

"Not really," the five-year-old said, shaking her small, *kapped* head. "I've ridden it a few times. It's not that hard to learn."

Mark only hoped he could ride the kick scooter with something close to Abby's coolness.

"Okay," he said, forcing himself to speak with enthusiasm, "let's get started with the lessons."

"You put your hands here," Jeremiah repeated himself, his patience very clear, "and rest them there to help you keep balance."

"I've seen these—" Mark said, "—they're faster than the *Englischer* scooters."

"*Yah*, faster because the tires are bigger."

Standing beside the scooter, he tested his foot in the cradle, which was on the small side for his feet. He noted also that the handlebars were lower and guessed that this particular scooter must have not been made for adults. It didn't matter. He had to learn to ride it.

Trying to focus totally on the scooter in front of him—and not on the *Maedel* on the haystack--Mark rested his hand on the handlebars, rocking the scooter side-to-side to feel the balance. "Okay. I should just take off right here?"

Jeremiah glanced around the area beside the barn. "*Yah*. This is *gut* for starting out. Give it a little push forward and see if you can jump on."

Bracketing his hands on the bar, Mark moved the scooter forward several feet, just to see how the thing worked. "Okay."

Giving the kick scooter a push, he trotted several feet forward and tried to shift his foot onto it.

From Sarah's vantage point on the stack of hay beside the barn, she watched Mark's jogging first attempts, noting that the scooter was short for him. It was interesting to see calm, always-in-control, laughing Mark doing something at which he wasn't yet totally competent.

In the next few minutes, he got it, though. With a few false starts, some stumbling missteps and one fall—from which he'd bounced up—and some wobbling around, he managed to get on the scooter and stay there for several yards.

"Hey! That was pretty good!" he hollered, jumping off the scooter as it wobbled to a stop.

"*Yah*!" responded Jeremiah, seeming excited that his friend was now more excited.

"I've got to try that again!"

Sarah watched the tall, lithe form as Mark ran, jumped onto the scooter and rode it a little further and faster than before. She should have known he would learn to ride the thing so quickly, given the skill with which he played physical games.

"This is fun," he gasped, coming to a stop in front of the haystack, "but I have to say, Jeremiah, that it's not as much fun as horses and buggies. You should spend some time with me in your *Daed's* buggy shop."

"Didn't your *Grossdaddi* run the buggy shop?" she asked, shaking hay off her skirts now that she'd come off the haystack.

"He did," Jeremiah said. "My *Daed* took it over after *Grossdaddi* and *Grossmammi* moved to the *Dawdy Haus* in Albona with my *Mamm's* brother and his wife."

"My father certainly thinks your *Daed* knows buggies," Sarah said. "We always come here when we need buggy work."

"Jeremiah here knows most everything about the shop, don't you?" Mark swiped the *Buwe's* straw hat, hanging just above where the child could reach. Rubbing Jeremiah's now-bare head, Mark said with an affection he'd been told wasn't always discernable, "I'm still new here, but Jeremiah has really helped me find my way."

Jumping to grab the hat Mark held above him, Jeremiah said between puffing breaths, "Like you haven't known my *Daed* and my *Mamm* before I was even here."

"I did know them. My own *Grossdaddi* introduced us when I was a troublesome scholar."

Knowing she should go back to wait for her *Daed* in the shop, Sarah instead sent Mark a grin with an edge. "You were troublesome? It's hard to believe."

He retorted back. "I'll bet it is. I'm so perfect now."

Looking up at him quickly, she twitched her eyebrows together, shooting back, "We are none of us perfect. *Gott* has recommended us not to judge other, certainly not as less."

"I never said I was perfect. You said that about me."

"That's not what I said, but I can see that you think so." Sarah glowered at him.

Laughing, Mark scooped up the jacket he'd tossed aside earlier. "You are funny."

Seeing that she'd get nothing from him other than this teasing, she turned and stomped away, her back rigid.

"*Neh*, I don't think I'm perfect," he called in a more serious voice as his voice became fainter with her departure. "I'm far from it, even if I did learn to ride the kick scooter in just a few tries."

Heading toward the buggy shop, Sarah stalked away, suddenly flushed. Why did this *Mann* make her so angry? One minute they were teasing and laughing and then he was suddenly arrogant and cocky.

Swiping at a tear that had escaped down her cheek—she hated crying when she was angry—Sarah reminded herself that *Gott* had directed them to be humble and kind to all. He'd also directed them to look at the plank of lumber in one's own eye, instead of the speck of dust in others' eyes.

Unable to keep her thoughts from swinging back to Mark and his frittering away of his good qualities, she muttered aloud to herself, "It's no matter to me!"

Arriving in the shop still flushed with anger—and other feelings that she didn't want to explore—she saw that her *Daed* was just shaking Daniel Stoltzfus' hand as he took his leave. "Thank you. I'll expect to bring the buggy back next week for refurbishing."

"Very *gut*," replied Daniel.

Walking toward the two, Sarah met Enoch as he came away. He smiled, seeming pleased at whatever he'd arranged. "Let's go *Dochder*. I've finished my errand here."

Minutes later, sitting on the buggy's driver box next to her *Daed*, she fell into silence, brooding over Mark and his arrogance that all would work out for him. This attitude didn't seem humble, as they were taught to be.

Of course, they'd also been taught to rely on *Gott's* love… It just seemed that *Gott* wanted them to do as much as they could.

Staring out at the passing farmland without seeing it, she brooded over Mark, a *Mann* who could make her laugh so hard—watching him learn to use the kick scooter had been very amusing—and then make her so angry.

Perfect! He really thought he could be so, as though any person could be without flaws.

When Enoch drove into their own yard, she saw Anna's buggy there and was glad to get to see her friend. To *Englischers*, all Amish buggies might look alike, but Sarah didn't fall into that category. She knew that Anna's new buggy—purchased just recently with some of the insurance settlement money—had brown wheels and a small, attached, barely-visible place to stick a flower.

Seeing the buggy there, Sarah was glad Anna was trying to create a life after the loss of her *Mamm*.

Now, if Mark could just decide on which kind of life he wanted to pursue!

CHAPTER NINE

"...and then Mark said he was perfect!" Sarah exclaimed sarcastically several days later as she rolled her eyes.

"He actually said that?" Anna asked. She was still apparently trying to get the picture. "This was when you were at the Stoltzfus' buggy shop in Elizabethtown with your *Daed*?"

"*Yah*," she answered, knowing her voice held an impatient edge. She and Anna stood at the back of the store while Jesse unloaded a supply wagon on the dock there with his young sons' help.

Little Eve and her faceless doll played several feet away.

"And this was when Lydia and Daniel's older boy taught Mark to ride a kick scooter?" Anna pursued with a wrinkled brow.

"*Yah*," Sarah responded with a laugh. "Do you know what that is?"

"Of course," Anna replied. "I've seen them ridden several times. Younger boys and *Menner*, mostly. Have you not seen them?"

Sarah shook her head. "I don't think I've seen them."

"They can get up to very high speeds! It seems a scary, but very efficient way to get around."

Giving a gurgle of laughter, Sarah said, "You should have seen him—Mark, I mean—he'd never ridden a scooter. It was funny to watch him learn, but that was before he got all bragging that he was perfect."

"That must have been strange, given that you watched him be a fool on that kick scooter."

"*Yah*, although, I have to say he picked it up pretty fast," Sarah admitted, suddenly struggling to banish from her mind the image of a shirt-sleeved *Mann*, all rumpled and dusty…and way too attractive. "It was so amusing to see him listening so seriously to Jeremiah and doing what the small *Buwe* told him to do."

"Jeremiah? That's Daniel and Lydia Stolzfus's son?"

"*Yah*. Their oldest. Their next, Abby, was sitting with me on a haystack as we watched."

"Oh." Anna nodded. "That must have been a lot of pressure for him. Mark, I mean."

"Pressure?" Sarah frowned. "What do you mean?"

"Well, to have an attractive *Maedel* and a little girl watch him learn to ride a scooter. I'd think he'd want to do that in private, is all I'm saying."

Still frowning, Sarah paused. She hadn't thought of the situation in just that way. "He didn't seem nervous."

"*Neh*, but haven't you told me that Mark doesn't show that kind of thing? That he's hard to read and seems to be teasing and laughing all the time?"

"*Yah*."

Anna shrugged. "I'm just saying that most *Menner* don't want to look foolish in front of attractive *Maedels*. And he actually said he's perfect?"

Looking down in thought, Sarah acknowledged, "Yes. He might have been teasing. It's hard to tell with him, but he said that. That he was perfect."

"I don't know," Anna got up, going to Eve to tuck the child's hair more securely under her black *Kapp*. "Nothing seems very clear between you two."

Saying nothing to this, Sarah brooded over her complex interaction with Mark. "He's not a usual sort of *Mann*."

Anna looked at her fixedly. "Are you… It seems like you like him."

She'd said something like this before and Sarah resorted to the response she'd claimed earlier. "Of course, I like him. We all went to school together."

"I mean you really like *like* him. As a *Mann*."

Sarah felt her cheeks flush. "I don't. I mean I don't think of him that way."

Raising her pale brows, Anna said, "You sound like maybe you do."

"I don't!" Sarah insisted. "He's not at all the sort of *Mann* I want to marry."

"His situation isn't what you want? Or you don't like him?"

Knowing she was getting redder, Sarah tried willing away the blush. She forced herself to speak calmly. "May I remind you that we all like Mark. He's a likeable kind of guy, as I've said before, but that's all."

"If you insist."

"I do!" she said in an emphatic voice. "He's nice, that's all."

"Okay."

Shifting on her seat, she forced herself to give Anna a smile, her friend's comment echoing loudly in her head.

"I'm just saying what it looks like," Anna said again brushing dirt off Eve, who'd come to stand in front of her, "but you know your own heart best."

"I do. *Denki*." She swallowed hard, the thumping in her chest having grown loud. Did she like him in that way? He annoyed her and had always made her want to shake him, but he made her laugh, too.

In a moment of brutal self-honesty, she looked down at her hands in her lap. Would she be jealous if he courted with or married someone else? If Mark married another girl, would she care?

The thumping in her chest getting louder in her ears, Sarah felt sick to her stomach at the thought of him standing beside another *Maedel* in front of the Bishop.

She—she did like *like* him. Sarah blinked back a sudden rush of tears. The thought of Mark marrying anyone but herself made her insides feel like a ball of stinging nettle.

In fact, despite all she knew about him, despite his disinterest in settling down and providing security for a *familye*, she loved Mark Fisher.

No wonder she had no interest in courting with any of the other *Menner* she knew.

Gulping in a breath, she admitted it to herself. She did. She loved Mark.

Wrestling with a bolt on the undercarriage of a buggy in for repairs a week after that, Mark nearly dropped the wrench on his chest when Abigail stuck her small head next to his.

"*Mamm* is here with lunch for you all."

"Good grief, girl!" he exclaimed. "Give a *Mann* some warning when you plan to pop in out of thin air."

"*Hallo*," she responded, her smile widening. "I didn't mean to startle you, but I thought you'd want lunch."

"I do want lunch." Mark scrambled out from under the buggy. "I'll go wash the grime off my hands."

As he stood at the water pump, lifting and pushing the handle, he saw two of Daniel and Lydia's younger children—only three and four, he'd guess—playing in a sand pile behind the buggy shop. Andrew and Matthew?

He'd been in and out of Daniel's shop since he was a sullen boy, come along with his *Grossdaddi*.

Daniel himself had taken a twisted journey to find *Gott*. He'd understood young, sullen Mark when it had seemed no one did.

"Come eat lunch!!" Lydia, Daniel's *Frau,* called as Mark walked out into the bigger room at the buggy shop. She wore a faded blue dress and stood stirring a pot of something, a chubby girl *Boppli* sitting on her hip. The *Boppli* had serious blue eyes and wore a small black *Kapp* on her head.

"Why so serious, baby Rachel?" he asked, reaching a newly-washed finger for her to grasp. "It is Rachel, isn't it? I'm pretty sure about her name, but the younger boys' names still escape me sometimes. I must be getting old."

Lydia laughed.

"I think you have to be older than twenty years to claim age as an excuse for anything and, yes, she is our Rachel," Lydia said, jiggling the *Boppli* a little. "Sweet little Rachel."

The baby, all chubby cheeks and pale, rosy skin, looked at him, a serious and faintly startled expression in her blue eyes.

"Your children are all so nice," he complimented her.

Lydia squinted a little. "How have you worked here this week and not met our elder two *Kinner*—Jeremiah and Abigail?"

He laughed. "I have met them and they're also nice. Nothing like I was as a *Buwe*, if you remember."

"I do remember," she said, chuckling with him. "I remember a surly, too-*schmaert*-for-his-own-good *Buwe*. A not-quite-ordinary boy."

"Let's just keep that not-quite-ordinary stuff to yourself."

She lifted her brows. "Why?"

"I like to sneak up on situations," he responded in a teasing voice. "People expect less of you if they don't think you're *schmaert*."

"I'm sorry," she said with a wry smile, "but you stand out like one of farmer Altorfer's sunflowers.

Hearing voices in the main area of the shop, he looked over to see Moses Blatter conferring there with Daniel. Members of their community were always in and out of Daniel's shop for buggy parts and repair. The appearance of Moses there was only remarkable because the *Mann* had a distinctive higher voice.

That, and Mark knew Moses had an interest in Sarah. He'd never made a secret of it.

"I like it here," Mark said abruptly to Lydia.

Clearly startled by his swift subject change, she said, "*Gut*. We're glad. We haven't seen enough of you lately."

He smiled. "I've missed you all, I've been busy working, but strictly speaking I meant that I like working here. Buggies are interesting."

"I'm glad," she responded. "You've certainly been around them since your *Grossdaddi* brought you here as a child."

"But there could be other work, other places that I can enjoy working."

She lifted her brows, "*Yah*. Of course."

Mark finished at the pump, drying his hands. "I'll be right in to eat."

"Great. Rachel and I will go set the food out."

Crossing the yard after Lydia, he cut across the buggy shop to where lunch had been laid out on a table.

"You're all washed up," Abby commented, appearing beside him to slip her small hand in his.

"I am," he agreed, picking her up so their faces were level. "Are you?"

"I am, too," she responded demurely, a cherubic smile on her fair face.

"Good girl." He slung her under his arm, walking to the lunch table.

"Put me down!" Abby squealed.

"Here?" he asked, stopping at the table.

"Yes!"

"Okay." Setting her down with minimal ruffling, Mark reflected that being here with Daniel and his *familye* felt like...almost like being home. He missed his twin, Grace, his *Eldre* and his younger siblings. His older brother was married and settled nearby while his younger *Geschwischder* were still at home. Grace would soon marry her Bart and the *Haus* would seem emptier, although young Benjamin, Claudia, Amity and Ezra made enough noise to fill it.

Mark had known Daniel, though, since he himself was a *scholar*. Daniel had reached out to him when Mark was a confused puppy.

Later, his older friend had told Mark that he was, at that time, confused himself, so Daniel had understood the experience. He seemed great now. Happily settled with Lydia and their brood, working here on vehicles, Mark, also, found interesting.

His throat tightened as he stood gathering his lunch, wondering if Sarah were right. Was it past time he settled down? Mark had to admit to himself that Daniel's life looked pretty good.

For a brief moment, he envisioned himself in a place like this...with Sarah at his side. She was pretty and sassy. He liked teasing with her. He had a totally wrong urge to catch her up in his arms and kiss her, but he didn't know.

He wasn't ready to secure himself to just one place.

"*Daed*," Joel tugged on his father's sleeve before the church service at the Yoder *Haus* a week later.

Scanning the crowded *Haus* for Grace and his *Eldre*, hoping they had empty chairs, Jesse shifted little Eve in his arms to looked down at Joel. Even though the windows were open to allow air circulation, the rooms were already warm with chattering bodies, as the service was about to start.

"*Daed*," Joel repeated. "can Levi and I sit with Jeremiah and Abby? Their *familye* is visiting from Elizabethtown."

"Is your *Onkle* Mark with them? Maybe you can sit by him," Jesse responded, looking for his brother's tall, muscular frame.

"*Yah*," Joel said, patience in his small-boy voice. "*Onkle* Mark is back there with them in the corner."

Hearing suddenly Mark's laughter ringing out, Jesse spotted his *Bruder's* blond head in the direction Joel indicated.

In scanning the room, Jesse saw Anna sitting next to Sarah and her sister, a *Scholar* of eight or nine.

The side of his mouth kicked up as he looked at the younger Miller girl, who seemed to feel very important to be sitting with the other two, older *Maedels*.

Jesse lost all desire to smile, though, when he noticed two young *Menner* next to Anna—one sitting next to her and another standing next to them, talking to her. Moses Graber and Saul Beiler?

Aware of staring at them too long, Jesse felt his jaw tighten. Of course, her insurance settlement made her now a marriage option for many, but…she deserved better.

He looked down and then at his insistent son.

"We'll come back after the service and have lunch with you and Eve," Joel assured him.

"Okay." Jesse drew in a deep breath, not realizing he was frowning at the *Buwe* until Joel said nervously, "Are you sure you don't mind? I'll keep an eye on Levi."

Forcing himself to smile at his son, he assured Joel. "*Gut*, you two go sit with your friends."

Hitching Eve a little more securely in his arms, he made his way to sit with his parents, Grace and his younger *Geschwischder*. Mark seemed to have settled into a spot with the Stoltzfus *familye*.

As others were all settling down, conversations were dying off as the meeting started.

Jesse sat down next to Grace, not happy that Anna and her fickle suitors were right in his eye line. He took a deep breath.

Anna deserved to have a husband and *familye* of her own.

He thought back on all she'd endured. Little exchanges between them during the time she'd watched over Joel, Levi and Eve had given him a pretty good idea of her life. She was such a good person and had suffered some very unfair challenges, what with her husband having deserted her and her *Mamm* dying in that accident.

He looked down again, keeping his face blank as he adjusted Eve on his lap.

That Anna had lived in this town with her *Mamm*, ignored by these same *Menner* who now made up to her, made him angrier than he could remember in a while. Maybe they were *gut* men— *Gott* saw the heart, but he couldn't. Regardless, Jesse needed to say nothing in response to their sudden courtships.

Swallowing a bitter taste in his mouth as he imagined watching Anna stand before the congregation to take a new husband, Jesse knew he had no right to this reaction. He had no claim on her.

Looking at her sitting with them, her white *Kapp* pinned close to her head, her hands folded in her lap, Jesse thought about Anna's kindness, her sweet attentions to his young *familye*. Even when he'd felt disconnected and lost, his grief and his focus on starting a new life, seeming to block him from those around him, even then he'd felt comfortable with Anna.

At peace.

Stupid *Menner*, not to see her value.

Rather than raise a ruckus about the unfairness of all of this to Anna , it was better to and focus on his own situation. He'd been recommended to look at his own situation, to make a new family.

Determined to ignore the spectacle in front of him, Jesse stared instead at the bishop leading the service.

He needed to attend to his own life and get out of Anna's way. She would be a great wife to any *Mann* who was so honored and, if her settlement led to her suddenly having choices of husband, he couldn't get in her way.

Even though, he badly wanted to.

Across the crowded Yoder *Haus,* Anna looked down at her sweaty hands, clasped in her lap.

"Perhaps I could take you for a ride in my new buggy sometime this week," Moses Graber said in a lowered voice from his seat next to her.

Before Anna could respond, Saul Beiler—standing right in front of her—said as the service was starting, "I'll just sit here, next to you."

Nodding as he took the seat on the other side of Moses, no longer trying to keep her attention, Anna looked attentively at the bishop giving today's talk.

His words went over her today, though.

This was all so strange—having *Menner* clamor around her. Even as a young *Maedel*, she'd never been this popular. Anna knew that her newfound wealth now attracted attention to her, but she couldn't find it in her to care what either Moses or Saul said. She'd gone to school with both and they'd both ignored her after Hiram left. This was hard to forget.

Across the room, she saw Jesse with little Eve in his arms.

His presence brought a swift smile to her face, but this dimmed as she gazed at his flat, stoic expression. Jesse looked almost…angry and she didn't know what to make of it.

Her gaze falling to her lap, Anna searched through her memories of the past several days, trying to think of anything she might have inadvertently done to earn his displeasure. Honestly, being with Jesse and the *Kinder* had been her quiet in the storm. She'd felt at peace there with them, glad she could help out and bathing in the sense of being valued and appreciated.

Falling into fond reminiscence, she found herself wishing she were sitting next to Jesse and Eve, rather than next to Moses and Saul. Even with his angry face, Jesse was a better option.

Just at that moment, she spotted Bart Zook across the room, smiling at her.

Anna quickly dropped her gaze. She'd rather liked Bart when they were back in school together but he'd acted, since Hiram's departure, like he also couldn't see her. Only this seemed to have changed for him. She couldn't acquit him of being like the others and that left her depressed.

Now, she really wanted to sit next to Jesse and Eve.

"I know Saul and Moses are morons, but you always liked Bart," Sarah said in an encouraging voice several days later. "Surely, if Bart asked you to be his *Frau*, you would be happy."

Her friend broke out in laughing protest. "I wouldn't say that Moses and Saul are *Debiels*, just foolish and not so reliable, I think."

"But Bart's not foolish and he always seemed reliable."

"I did like him in school," Anna admitted, "but I can't help think worse of him given his behavior towards me after Hiram left."

Sarah shrugged, saying to her kind-hearted friend, "*Yah*. I can see that his ignoring you all this time would be hard to forget."

The two sat on Sarah's front porch, the sun rising high in the sky. Both had finished their chores for the day and were now visiting when two buggies pulled into the driveway that curved in front of the *Haus*.

The girls stopped speaking, both looking at the vehicles. Enoch, Sarah's *Daed*, drove the first one, but the other buggy had to pull up behind this before they could see that Mark drove it.

And, Sarah noticed, something seemed to have upset him. Her normally-smiling Mark wore a dark scowl when he looked her way.

Not that he was her Mark.

Oddly enough, though, he greeted Anna—who had gone to the porch steps—with non-hostile pleasantries. Realizing that his hostility was aimed solely at her, her welcoming smile faded.

He was mad at her for some reason?

Sarah felt her gaze go frosty, the inside of her suddenly cold. She hated him being mad at her, while, at the same time, she couldn't see why this should be so.

"Is this your new buggy, Mr. Miller," Anna called to Enoch.

"*Neh!*" He laughingly waved. "I've not bought it, yet. Got to trot it around and discuss the case with Kate."

"I would think so!" Anna laughed in response.

"Come." Enoch gestured for all to follow him into the *Haus*, "Kate! Kate!"

With the others disappearing inside, Sarah looked at Mark.

He'd driven her *Daed's* buggy up behind the one Enoch had brought home to try out.

Sarah's chin lifted to a militant angle, she got in the first shot—bitterness and grief fueling her words. "What are you doing here?"

It was hard to see, right in front of her, what she wanted and know she'd never have it...because he was a jerk!

"As you can see," Mark gestured toward the buggy with a twitch of his head, "I brought your *Daed's* buggy."

"That doesn't seem very necessary. If you'd left it at the buggy shop in Elizabethtown, he could have gotten it when he returned the new buggy."

"Maybe this is lost on you," he snapped, "but this way, your *Daed* will find it more difficult to return the new buggy and is more likely to buy it."

Straightening at the anger in his voice, she ignored the urge to stick out her tongue, glaring at him instead. "Whatever has you in such a tizzy?"

His jaw tightening, Mark finished tying off the buggy reins to the buggy before he turned to her.

"I'd like to know, Sarah, what gives you the right to speak to Daniel about me?"

"What?" Thrown off-kilter, she widened her eyes, a sickening sinking in her middle. "I don't know what you mean."

"What gives you the right to speak to Daniel about me?" He repeated, his words not louder, but said them with a furious crispness.

"I didn't," she stammered, "I didn't. What do you mean?"

She was afraid that she knew exactly what he meant, though.

Her belly roiling more as the seconds passed, Mark asked, "Are you saying then, that Daniel made it up when he told me that you suggested he should 'convince' me to stay working with him?"

"Oh." Sarah felt herself flush as she prodded herself to think fast. "Of course, Daniel and I speak. You saw me there with my *Daed* just the other day."

"This was," his tone was no less angry for having dropped a level or two, "not the average conversation, apparently."

"Oh."

"That's right," Mark climbed down from the buggy box, coming around to stand right in front of her. "He told me that you'd talked to him and Daniel recommended that I be more open with my future *Frau*!"

Sarah felt the blood drain from her cheeks, her voice trembling as she said, "I-I never said anything about being your future *Frau*! Not specifically."

"You didn't?"

Seeing the doubt on his face, she insisted hotly, "*Neh*! I didn't!"

Now wasn't the time to outline exactly what she'd said.

Mark plainly wasn't convinced. "He seemed pretty clear about it."

"All I said—and totally in passing—was that you looked to never settle down and that I thought any *familye* you had would suffer." When he said nothing to this, Sarah lifted her chin again. "I said nothing to him that I've not said to you! Can you tell me that you see yourself settling down?"

"That is not your business, Sarah. It's mine and *Gott's*!" His voice was openly furious now. "You had no right to talk about this, at all, and certainly not to Daniel."

Gesturing as though to push away his words, she said in a tone that was regrettably evasive, "It wasn't like that. I didn't tell Daniel that we were to marry—not in those words, anyway—and I didn't tell him to make you stay!"

"*Neh*? Well, what did you say?" he snapped. "'He was certainly under the impression that we were courting and that you had asked him to convince me to settle down in the buggy shop!"

With deep embarrassment and a half-hearted plea for *Gott* to snatch her from the Earth right then, she cleared her throat. "Well, I remember that we discussed how warm the weather…and talked generally of what our friends are doing…"

Obvious skepticism on his face, he said, "But that wasn't all. Was it?"

"No, we talked also of the new buggy…" Sarah couldn't bring herself to meet his angry gaze.

"And me, too, it seems. You discussed me. You indicated that you and I plan to marry. At least, Daniel was convinced that this was what you meant. You think you know what is best for me, Sarah? That I should work here with Daniel and not move to another job?"

Her ire rising as he spoke, she retorted, "Well, you seemed happier here in the buggy shop with Daniel and Lydia and their *Kinder*."

Mark stepped closer. "And it is your job to determine my choices? To decide where I'm happiest? *Gott* directed you to do this?"

"Of course, not," she snorted. "What a ridiculous thing to say."

"But that is what you did, isn't it? You suggested that Daniel—you told him to talk me into staying. You told him this."

"Not exactly! I don't think I used those words exactly! I think I just mentioned that you seemed happy here."

"I'm happy anywhere!" he thundered, not sounding at all happy.

"Not as happy as in the buggy shop. You seem happier here," she replied, mulishly holding on to her position.

As voices could be heard with individuals coming out onto Enoch and Kate's porch, he lowered his voice, saying with the same intensity, "This is not your work, Sarah. It's not your right to talk to anyone about me."

"No," she agreed, abject misery coating her insides, "No, of course not."

She knew she was about to burst into tears and wished intensely that she were face-down on her bed, able to give vent to the emotions that choked her. Sarah wasn't alone, however.

Lifting her chin again, she said in a hard voice, "You're right. *Gott* wants each of us to find our own paths. You have every right to this...and so do I."

...

CHAPTER TEN

Sarah sorted through the bin of onions in a basket near the register. It didn't help to have time for her mind to wander while her hands were busy. She just couldn't stop running over and over the conflict she'd had with Mark.

The jerk. How could she have let such a *dumm hund* even disturb her thoughts?

He just wouldn't listen!

Sarah sniffled.

The store was now empty of customers, the morning rush having died off. Soon, the middle of the day customers would come in, but silence surrounded her now.

Jesse was back in his office, seeming as if he were as deep in thought as her.

Sarah's thoughts drifted back to Mark and another wave of sadness shook her, quickly followed by anger.

As she was wrestling with these emotions, Jesse came out of his office, closely examining a ledger he kept on a shelf under the register to record debts owed by customers who paid at the end of the month.

Sorting now through some apples and oranges, kept by the register for hungry *Kinder*, she noted after a few minutes that neither had said anything. The silence between them didn't bother her as much as it normally would, as she wasn't in the mood to make idle chit chat.

Her thoughts returning to her marital choices, Sarah firmed her jaw and began to sort through the *Menner* in their church who were thought to be looking for wives. Of course, a number of them about her age were already courting with *Maedels*. She probably should be, as well, but she'd never had a desire to spend more time with any of the *Buwes* in her class at school. Lots of *Mamms* with *Dochders* of marriageable age would have been nudging their girls by this time, but Kate never did, bless her.

The only time she'd ever mentioned Sarah's marriage was to say that she wanted her *Dochdar* to marry a *Mann* who fit into her heart.

Sarah swallowed a sob. She didn't have that option, though, as the *Mann* who fit into her heart was being a jerk.

Jesse closed the ledger with a snap just then. "The store seems quiet when no one is here."

Looking at him a minute, Sarah wasn't in the mood just now to tease him about his lame remark. All she said was, "*Yah*."

Each still locked in their thoughts, silence again settled over the place. It was then that Sarah noted her boss seemed as depressed in his reflections as she felt.

There was a mid-morning flurry of customers before silence again settled over the store.

"Has Anna been in with the children?" Jesse asked, looking around as if one was about to jump out at him.

"She was here briefly an hour ago when we had half-dozen others in the store," she said in a dispirited voice.

"Oh." He said before relapsing again into his thoughts.

Engaged in wiping down the counter by the register, she was startled when he abruptly spoke again.

"The bishops, and even my *Bruder*, think I should marry again. The *Kinder* need a *Mamm* and I need a partner in life."

It was her turn to say, "Oh."

"Every *Mann* deserves a helpmate," Jesse said doggedly, sounding completely unenthusiastic about the prospect.

"He does," Sarah said after a few moments. Here he was—a *Mann* who had a *gut* business. A *Mann* whose *familye* would never go hungry or be left to the kindness of friends if he died. She had thought of Jesse when looking about her for a husband who met her requirements. She ought to be, she knew, overjoyed to hear him say these words to her.

She just couldn't work up any enthusiasm, though.

The two went about their work in between serving the occasional customer. For a while, Jesse sat back in the office doing book work, she supposed.

Later that afternoon, he came out, pausing in the short hallway as he scanned the store, which was then empty.

Stocking some items at the end of an aisle, she glanced at him, vaguely noticing that his expression seemed both set and determined.

"Sarah? Would you come up here?"

She got to her feet and wiped her dusty hands on the back of her apron before hurrying to the counter. "Do you have a job for me?"

"Do you like my *Kinder*?"

His blunt question was unexpected.

"*Yah*. Very much," she responded, confused at the direction of the conversation. "I've enjoyed spending time with them and Anna. We even took them to Mr. Altorfer's sunflower patch where they liked walking carefully amongst the tall flowers."

Jesse looked down, pausing for several minutes. "You know that my Hannah, my *Frau*, died several years ago?"

"Yes," she said, still mystified by the direction of his questions.

"It is time…" His jaw hardened. "*Gott* has said it is not *gut* for man to be alone. It is time for me to choose another helpmate."

Sarah felt herself go still, her eyes widening. Inside her chest, her heart beat a slow, heavy rhythm.

"*Yah*."

"I think," he said, "that you and I work well together. Don't you think we work well here at the store?"

"I do," she responded, startlingly aware at that moment that even though she'd thought of Jesse as a *Mann* who fit her needs, she didn't feel for him anything like she did for his *Bruder*.

As annoying as she found him to be, Mark made her laugh and feel like killing him and...and want to have his babies. Not Jesse, the one she should have been thrilled to marry.

"I think," Jesse said, looking down at his hands, "we could make a good life together, you and I."

For the life of her, Sarah couldn't form the words to agree with him. He was right, of course. It was her life plan to have *Kinder* and a reliable husband. Jesse was reliable, she reminded herself in frustration.

"We don't know one another very well yet, but I know that you're honest, dependable and kind." Jesse looked anything but enthused as he described her.

Ducking his head again, Jesse said, "I will not lie to you, Sarah. I am still...dealing with...Hannah's death, but I know that *Gott* will help me and I'll be able to move on one day. In the meantime, my children need a *Mamm*."

It flashed through Sarah's mind that he was a good *Mann* and that maybe he was being more honest with her than she'd been with him.

"I do like Joel, Levi and little Eve. Every time I've spent with Anna and the *Kinner*, they've been very nice," she said slowly, struggling with the jarring sensation of finding herself in her ideal situation and it not seeming at all ideal.

Jesse nodded decisively. "I thought so. So, it is settled between us? Of course, mentioning it just yet would be like bragging. We'll wait till later in the summer and then be married this fall when the crops are in."

She resisted the urge to jerk back as if slapped in the face. *No one will know for weeks*, the thought whispered through her head. "*Yah*. Okay."

Right now, she couldn't imagine telling anyone about their proposed marriage. Not even Kate or Sarah's younger sister, Elizabeth.

Or Mark. She definitely couldn't tell Mark,

"Will you tell your *familye*?" she whispered. On the one hand, Jesse doing it would spare her. On the other, she didn't want Mark hearing of this now.

"Maybe," Jesse replied. "Maybe in a few weeks."

Lots could happen in a few weeks. Lots. Maybe Jesse would grow on her, becoming more like his brother. Maybe Mark would be so torn up at losing her to his *Bruder* that he stayed in Elizabethtown, as she'd hoped before.

Sarah sniffled back a tear, noting that Jesse was so caught up in his thoughts, he didn't notice.

Maybe she would fall dead and sleep in *Gott's* loving arms for eternity. That sounded really good about now.

Ever since he'd decided to not get in Anna's way and to marry some other *Maedel*, Jesse couldn't stop thinking about her. Even thoughts of Hannah seemed faded when he was with Anna. Sitting at the kitchen table with his children and her two days after having proposed to Sarah, he clamped down on his attraction to the soft-spoken woman now serving oatmeal into his *Kinner's* bowls.

"Are you keeping busy at the store?" she asked with her gentle smile, pausing to wipe cereal off Eve's face.

"*Yah*," he replied. "Seems I like a saw you there with young Bart Zook."

She looked down at her plate. "I did run into him on my way to your store."

"You…ran into him?"

"*Yah*."

Jesse observed that she looked more stressed than happy about the occurrence, chastising himself for his pleased satisfaction at this. He wanted the best for Anna, but he couldn't see her happily married to Bart or any of the local *Menner*. This wasn't his decision, of course. *Gott* would guide her best. Jesse just needed to stay out of the matter.

"I have to get to the store," he said abruptly, the happiness of the morning seeming to have drifted away.

"Of course." Anna smiled at him as she said this, his insides going all mushy.

Nodding and brushing his hand across Levi's blond head, he walked out.

Jesse launched himself into his buggy a few minutes later to pick up the reins and direct the horse down the drive. All the way to the store, he mulled over his dilemma. He just needed to commit himself more firmly to this marriage. Maybe it was time to move forward with everything.

Mark whistled as he drove toward his *Bruder's* store in Mannheim. He liked coming home to Mannheim to see his *Eldre* and his *Geschwischder*, especially Grace. She was to marry and move to her own home soon and he felt compelled to visit more because of this.

Of course, going to Jesse's store meant he would see Sarah and that really brightened his day, despite their recent ugly conversation. Parking his buggy under a tree and putting a pail of water close to his horse's head, he strode into the store.

Only one customer was inside this morning, standing at the front counter across from Jesse. Registering in an absent way that his brother looked more serious than usual, Mark scanned the store rows to find Sarah kneeling in front of a display to the side.

He stood there with a grin on his face, watching her stock the shelves, shifting the products carefully to make each more appealing. She hadn't noticed his entrance and therefore didn't react to his presence.

Behind him, the bell on the door jangled as Jesse's customer left.

"*Hallo Bruder.*"

It occurred to him more forcefully then, that Jesse seemed especially severe that morning.

At her boss' words, Sarah swiveled around, her face also different than usual. He couldn't say how, but she didn't give him her usual comical sigh or roll her eyes at him.

He'd come to love her exasperated sighs.

"I didn't know you were in Mannheim," Jesse said.

"I rode over from Daniel's buggy shop for a visit."

Mark looked between Sarah and Jesse, registering with a narrowing of his eyes that they both seemed tense for some reason. Could his *Bruder* have said harsh words to his employee and he interrupted the scolding?

Jesse drew in a long breath. "I'm glad you have come."

"Yes?" Looking back and forth at them, Mark wasn't sure what was going on.

Then, his *Bruder* crossed the space and put out a hand to Sarah to help her to her feet.

She looked startled, her throat moving as she swallowed awkwardly.

What was going on with these two, he wondered as they stood before him, looking uncomfortable.

"*Yah.*" Jesse held on to Sarah's hand, but the gesture didn't look like he'd done it often. "It gives me the chance to tell you that Sarah here has agreed to become my *Frau* and *Mamm* to my *Kinder.*"

Mark stared at the two in shock. Sarah to marry Jesse?

"What?"

His brother's announcement seemed to have surprised Sarah, but she didn't protest the words or correct him.

"Are you serious?" Mark heard the harshness in his voice, but couldn't find it in himself to gentle the question.

"We are," Jesse said. "We will marry this fall when the harvest is in."

Feeling suddenly flushed with anger and, at the same moment, as if he were hollow inside, Mark repeated in disbelief. "You two are to marry? Truly?"

Rage pounded in his head and he felt like throwing up.

"We are," Sarah confirmed, sounding almost angry. "Are you saying we should not?"

Responding to her defiant question with a stare, he looked at them in disbelief. Sarah didn't love Jesse. Nor Jesse love Sarah. That was obvious.

"Can you tell me why you would marry one another?" Mark asked, his words coming out clipped.

"Is it not *Gott's* wish that each should have an earthly partner?" She shot the question at him, turning to step closer to his *Bruder* to place her hand on Jesse's arm with obvious deliberation.

Not having said anything after his announcement, Jesse actually looked startled by her show of affection, glancing back and forth between Mark and Sarah.

"Can there be a reason why we should not marry?" His brother seemed to be serious in his question. As if he were open to this possibility.

It flashed through Mark's head that he could demand Jesse not marry her because Mark himself loved Sarah. The thought streaked past, but Mark didn't want to examine it closely. Shouldn't Jesse have a wife who loved him. "When I recommended you to marry again, I didn't mean you had grab the first *Maedel* you saw and rush into it."

Sarah jerked around to look at Mark, her expression stormy. "It is not up to your brother to determine who you should marry! It is our own business, only open for *Gott's* direction."

Jesse stared at her, his face showing confusion and hesitancy. "*Yah.* This is true."

She turned toward Mark again. "This isn't your business and your views aren't necessary here."

His jaw hardened and his mouth tightened as he tried to hold back words he knew he shouldn't say. Sucking in a breath, he asked his brother, "You want this? Marriage to Sarah?"

Jesse's gaze fell after a few minutes. "*Gott* has directed us to marry and bring *Kinner* into the world."

"That He did, but each of us ourselves chooses who to marry." Mark knew his words were said in a tense voice, but he didn't care.

This couldn't be.

Sarah didn't love Jesse, Mark knew in his heart, and his brother deserved that.

"Well," she declared in that same defiant, angry voice, "we've chosen to marry one another."

The three stood frozen in a silent tableau, Jesse's gaze having fallen as the other two glared at one another.

"You know this is wrong," Mark said to her, almost as if the two of them were alone.

Sarah dropped her hand from Jesse's arm, taking an impetuous step toward Mark. "You know what is wrong? Wasting the talents *Gott* gave you! Moving from job to job rather than settling in to make a life!"

Their gazes dueled and, not wanting to explore the hollow feeling in his chest, Mark shot back at her, "You have your own reasons for this marriage, but you should consider if this will make my brother happy."

Finding himself perilously close to saying hasty words that needed be said, Mark snapped. "You do as *Gott* directs you."

With those words, he turned and strode out of the store, stopping as his impetuous steps led him to the porch that ran the length of the building. He looked blindly at the parking area. It was as if the world around him had shifted to black and gray, everything looking different.

His heart pounded against his ribs and Mark realized, as the slight breeze shimmered past, that he'd broken into a sweat during the confrontation.

This was so wrong…and Sarah knew it, even if Jesse were just trying to move forward. Sarah knew she didn't love him.

Mark suddenly stood stock still, stopping on the steps leading to the parking area.

In that, he felt himself go bone-chilling cold. As icy cold now as he'd been heated before.

He loved Sarah. He loved her. He'd have been angered and distressed at whoever she married,

He loved her. This wasn't really anything to do with his brother, other than the truth that Jesse and his children deserved more than a woman hiding from the world.

As mad, as furious as he was with her—Mark wanted to shake her—he also wanted to crush her in his arms, rain kisses on her face and remind her that she was strong enough, with *Gott's* guidance, to handle anything in this life.

Mark gulped in a breath, finishing the few steps to the parking lot.

He wanted to shake her really hard...and at the same time he was determined that Jesse wouldn't marry Sarah. He didn't know how he'd keep this from happening, but he would.

Sarah walked home after work that day, entering Enoch and Kate's farm through a back path that crossed through several fields and over a footbridge before the *Haus* came into view. As the summer was now at its height, the air around her was warm. The walk from work to home was, of course, a familiar one, and generally this was a time she enjoyed as she trekked past green fields and over the bubbling creek.

Today, all she could think about was the horrible mess into which she'd gotten herself. She'd had no idea Jesse had decided to tell Mark about their marriage until he'd blurted it out.

She hadn't told her *Eldre*, hesitant to say the words out loud.

Her footstep made a hollow sound when she stepped onto the wooden footbridge that crossed the stream, her head was down, thoughts circling.

Looking up just then, she saw Mark standing on the footbridge, glaring at her.

Coming to a sudden halt, she clutched at the cloth bag over her shoulder, her lunch containers inside making a rustling sound as they came together.

"How could you do this to Jesse?" He spat the words out, looking more furious than she'd ever seen him...and she'd seen Mark angry several times.

"I don't know what you mean," she responded, her voice more defensive than it should have been. At the sight of him, her insides jumped and her heart beat faster in her chest.

"You know he's grieving!"

Sarah stiffened her backbone, reminding herself that Mark hadn't indicated any interest in her...even if she did love him. She owed him nothing. "You and the bishop told Jesse he should marry again!"

"To a *Maedel* who holds his heart! He feels nothing for you!"

"What do you mean? How do you know Jesse feels nothing for me?" she shot back, bridling at his arrogant inference, her chest still thumping with a combination of her feelings for him— including anger at his anger.

"I'm his brother," Mark responded in a nasty voice. "*Menner* talk, you know? I have never heard him utter your name. You mean that little to him."

"You may be his *Bruder*, but that doesn't mean he tells you everything," Sarah said, her tone scathing. Not even sure why she was engaging with him in this, a little voice in her head reminded her that she herself wasn't totally comfortable with her decision.

"Have you even thought of Joel, Levi and Eve?"

"I have," she insisted. "I'll be a good mother!"

"One that doesn't love their father! How can that be *gut* for them?"

"How would you know this?" she shot back, lost in fighting with him, her breath coming faster.

"Jesse deserves better," Mark went on as if she'd said nothing. "His *Kinder* deserve better."

"Are you saying," she demanded, "that I'm somehow not good enough for Jesse?"

"I'm saying," Mark responded, "that I had no idea how far you'd go to win our bet."

144

"What!?" she gasped out the word. "I barely even remember our bet!"

Still apparently deaf, he ground out, "I had no idea of how far you'd go, but it's clear now!"

"You know nothing about me!" She was so furious that her breath came in short pants. "And what of you? As I remember, you claimed that you would settle into one work! Somewhere! Find your spot and become the kind a *Mann* that a *Maedel* could rely on!"

"Don't you worry about me," he said. "I have no issue getting or keeping a job. This isn't your concern."

"Oh, you can get work and you could keep a job, if you just would!"

"Never you mind," he said furiously, stepping closer to her in his anger. "You need only concern yourself with your own problems."

"I don't have any!" She squared up to him, so angry as she glared right back into his blue eyes. "I'm marrying and not to a risky, care-for-nobody *Mann* like you!"

"I never asked you to marry me, despite what you told Daniel."

"*Aarrghhh!*" So mad she could hardly see straight, she stormed past him, stomping across the footbridge, Mark's words following her.

"Remember! *Gott* has instructed us to be kind. Are you being kind to Jesse?"

The next morning, Jesse came slowly into his kitchen, hearing the cheerful sounds of his *Kinder* talking and laughing with Anna.

He hadn't slept well the night before, turning and bunching his pillow under his head.

After deciding impulsively to tell Mark about his plans to marry again, he kept replaying different scenes in his head. Mark had told him directly to get another *Frau*. His *Bruder* was *schmaert*, so he'd listened. Having made his announcement as much to commit himself further to an action that still disturbed him, he'd told Mark about Sarah and himself. Making the announcement, however, hadn't jarred him into feeling better about his future.

Shouldn't he be more excited? He'd been excited and happy to marry Hannah.

Jesse had a headache.

He paused at the kitchen doorway, a faint smile ghosting over his face as he observed Anna with the three small people at the table.

Levi saw him first. "*Daed*! Come have breakfast. Anna made pancakes and some fried taters!"

"I know you love both," Jesse said, ruffling his son's blond hair as he pulled out a chair. "I'm late, Anna. Can I just have a cup of coffee?"

Her smile just about broke his heart. "Of course! I'll get it for you right away."

The sight of her brightened what had been, till then, a gray morning. Jesse sat in his chair, staring at her, feeling as if struck by a bolt of lightning.

He loved Anna! He loved her. This was why he'd decided, after seeing how she was treated before, not to in any way impede her finally getting her due. He wanted the best for her because he loved Anna.

Automatically cradling the warm mug she sat before him a moment later, Jesse wondered why he hadn't realized this before. True, he didn't feel for her the *Youngie* crush that he'd felt for Hannah. This burning inside him was—he recognized now—the passion of a grown *Mann*.

He couldn't imagine marrying anyone but Anna. Certainly not the woman to whom he'd spoken of marriage just the day before.

Jesse swallowed hard, staring into the steaming drink in his mug. What did an honorable *Mann* do now?

What an idiot he'd been!

Slammed back into the moment by his older son pushing his chair under the table, Jesse realized several things at once. All three of his *Kinner* were gone from the kitchen, the last just disappearing through the door. Since chores were usually accomplished before breakfast, he didn't know where they were heading or even if they'd told him, but gone unheard while he was so deep in thought.

Anna pulled out the chair Joel had occupied, seating herself across from Jesse.

Just the sight of her gentle, sweet face smiling at him brought a responding smile to Jesse's face.

"I understand," Anna said softly, "that you are to marry Sarah."

His mouth suddenly dry, he could think of nothing to say.

"I wish you both much happiness." She smiled at him, her mouth seeming to quiver briefly.

He stared at her a moment, saying nothing.

Curving her hands around her own mug, Anna said in a determined voice, "Sarah has been a very great friend all my life. She deserves the best and I'm sure you fit this bill."

"She told you?" Jesse finally blurted out the words in a harsh voice, suddenly angrier than he had any right to be. Afterall, he'd announced to Mark that they were to marry.

Staring at him as if startled, Anna said hesitantly, "*Yah.*"

Jesse lowered his gaze to the table, knowing he needed to regain some self-control, but struggling. Infuriated that the happiness he knew he'd have had married to Anna was being snatched from him even as he identified what was in his bones. How could he marry Anna now?

"Sarah and I are friends," she said, looking mystified at his reaction. "She just wanted to share her joyful news."

"Of course." Jesse wrestled with himself. Anna's words were supportive...almost as if she was glad to see him marry someone else.

Anna's smile seemed forced, but that could be wishful thinking on his part.

They hadn't been courting. He not only hadn't spoken to her of marriage, he knew he'd not acted particularly interested in her. She worked in his home with his children. If she didn't return his feelings, everything would have been awkward. Jesse knew his reaction made no sense, but he didn't see how his feelings for her could be this strong without her having some interest in him.

Stretching her smile to where it was broader—and yet didn't reach her eyes—she said, "I think you marrying again is a good thing."

"You do?" More than anything, he wanted her to say yes, she did want him to marry, but to marry her, not Sarah.

Taking a breath, she broke the silence that had fallen between them. "I—I want you to be happy, too. And the children need a *Mamm* to smother them with kisses and help them water the garden."

"You do those things with them," Jesse said, his voice husky.

A gentle smile curved her pink mouth, her blue gaze cast down so he couldn't fully read her expression. "*Yah*, I do, and I love them, but I want them to have a *Mamm* and more brothers and sisters. I want you—all of you—to be happy and to live righteous lives."

She glanced back up at him with an expression he couldn't read.

"Good," he said, grabbing his coat from the peg where it hung in a corner, "Good for you."

CHAPTER ELEVEN

Mark stared up at the buggy's dusty undercarriage. All he could think about was his argument with Sarah the day before. Another argument.

The shop was busy, as usual, full of vehicles in various stages of repair or restoration. At the end of the big, rectangular building, several workers talked as they stood near the office.

Cool here under the buggy, Mark let his hands drop from the back axle, staring blankly at the dark, dusty buggy floorboards above him. Sarah had agreed to marry Jesse.

Sarah married to another *Mann*.

Aware of the tightness in his chest, he again replayed the argument over and over in head, the other workers' conversation fading.

He and Sarah had certainly squabbled before, but this...this felt much bigger. Uglier.

Mark's mouth tightened as he thought of her married to his *Bruder*. He'd have to move away, of course, as the thought of seeing her at family gatherings...knowing she was pledged to another...knowing he could never have her...it wasn't bearable.

In his whole life, he hadn't been so empty inside. So...lost. He hated the thought of being so far from his *Eldre* and his *Geschwischder*. And Grace was marrying soon. Moving would mean that he wouldn't see her, or her eventual children, very often.

Her soon-to-be husband was a *gut* friend of his, as well. He'd miss his brother, too.

He couldn't, though, stay here and watch Sarah marry another, particularly his *Bruder*.

Why hadn't he realized…hadn't known till that moment that he loved Sarah? Bossy, maddening, irritating, wonderful Sarah.

Closing his eyes against the shaft of pain that went through him, Mark's thoughts spiraled and he found himself suddenly praying. *It's all a mess, Lord. I ask that you help me. I cannot stop thinking of her. Gott, I don't ask for help easily. You know this about me. I cannot do this on my own, Lord. Please help me.*

Feeling no bolt of lightning in response to his prayer, he did recognize that a sense of calmness had settled over him. He still didn't know what to do, but he sent up a prayer of gratitude that he wasn't alone.

Later that afternoon, Mark found himself working with Daniel on fitting cushions into a buggy that had been built in the shop from the wheels up.

"You seem quieter than usual." Daniel looked up from where he had been struggling to set the black pads in place in the passenger compartment.

Not able to think of a single lighthearted response, Mark admitted, "*Neh.*"

"What's making you so gloomy?" his friend asked after a moment of wrestling.

Mark looked down at the unfinished seats. "What do you remember from when I was young?"

Making no remark about the change in subjects, Daniel said promptly, "I remember that we were both lost. Your *Grossdaddi* had brought you by here when he came to pick up a buggy reflector, I think."

"*Yah.*"

"I remember that you were a surly youth, angry with everyone and giving your *Eldre* fits. That's why you were spending some time with your *Grossdaddi*."

"It was," Mark said, his brooding gaze unfocused.

"I introduced you to the mare, Apple, who needed some gentling, and we grew to be friends."

Nodding in two quick jerks of his head, Mark said, "*Yah*. You have been my very best friend, next to Grace."

Daniel stopped working at the buggy cushion, looking steadily at him. "You are troubled my friend. Can I help?"

Not responding for a few minutes, Mark finally said, his chest feeling heavy, "*Neh*, my friend. This time I have trouble with which no human can help me."

"That sounds pretty bad," Daniel commented, "and I don't think I've ever heard you speak with such despair."

"I don't think," he said after a moment, "that I've ever felt this miserable before."

"Ouch." His friend's face was somber.

"I keep praying to *Gott*, but I haven't yet been able to decipher His answer."

Daniel nodded before saying with simple invitation after a moment, "Is this about Sarah?"

Looking over at him quickly, he evaded. "Why do you assume that?"

Laughing, his friend said, "You seem different when she's here and when you talk about her all the time."

"I don't think I talked about her that much." He knew he sounded defensive, but that was just how the words came out of his mouth.

Just looking at him with a smile, Daniel shook his head.

Flushing, Mark mumbled, "…not that much."

"And then there's her having spoken to me about you."

"She had no right to do that!"

"Or to imply that there's an understanding between the two of you?"

"*Neh*." If there had been…if he had arranged to marry her, he wouldn't have this knife in his gut right now.

Continuing to coax the seats into the buggy interior, Daniel said, "Then there's just no understanding why she did."

"I spoke firmly to her about having talked to you about me," Mark inserted.

"Did you? That must have upset her. Do you remember that I told you she stammered and blushed when asking me to invite you again to join my business here?"

"I like working here with you… More than any other work I've done," he admitted.

"I'm glad. Very glad."

Handing his friend the last cushion to wedge into place, Mark stared out the buggy window. "I should have accepted your offer."

"*Yah?*"

"And asked Sarah to marry me." He looked fixedly at the seat next to where Daniel worked.

"*Yah?* This is what you want?"

"I've teased her and—and argued with her so much," Raising his gaze to his friend, he said in a low voice, "and now she's to—she's to marry someone else. My heart has been yanked through my chest."

"Oh, friend," Daniel responded, pausing his actions to say sympathetically. "I felt just the same with Lydia."

"And now it's too late." Mark heard the thickness in his own voice, feeling as desperate as, he remembered now, he'd told himself he would never feel.

The pit of her stomach roiling, the next morning, Sarah looked up from the breakfast dishes in the soapy water, knowing as her brothers, Joshua and Matthew, clattered out, that she needed to speak. With Jesse having made his announcement to Mark, the secret of their betrothal was out. Oh, it wasn't yet open knowledge, but she knew people talked. Even though they were forbidden from being boastful, this kind of thing usually got around. She didn't want her *Mamm* and *Daed* to hear the news from someone other than herself.

"*Mamm*," Sarah swallowed hard, "*Mamm*, I have news."

Kate had looked up from her dish drying. "*Yah*?"

Sarah knew that their friends and family didn't voice opinions about different unions. She almost wished they would, forbidding her to marry a *Mann* she didn't know well. Yes, she'd grown up in the same small schoolhouse as Jesse and Mark, but Jesse was older and had married Hannah to move away when Sarah was still a *Youngie*.

She knew Mark better, she thought inconsequently.

"I—I have agreed to marry Jesse Fisher," she finally blurted out baldly.

Her *Mamm* stared at her for a moment.

"You know," Sarah added, "the *Mann* for whom I work at Bontreger's—or I should say Fisher's—store?"

Kate still stared at her, a crinkle between her brows. "Oh! Yes, of course we know Jesse. Knew him as a *scholar*. I just didn't know...you were that close."

Feeling she had to in some way normalize this, Sarah said, "You know, we've seen a lot of one another since I started working there."

"Yes, you have," was Kate's response, her confused look not abating.

Picking up a dish from the soapy water, Sarah began cleaning it. "*Yah*. Jesse's doing everything to make the store turn a profit. You know he's carrying some new different livestock feeds now."

Her *Mamm* said nothing for a moment.

"You know," Sarah went on desperately, "he was widowed with three young *Kinder*. Anna's caring for them while he works. She brings them to the store sometime."

"Oh," Kate still seemed a little bemused, "so you know his children?"

"*Yah*," she forced herself to say in a chatty voice, feeling her cheeks flush warm, "you know that Jesse, Mark and his twin, Grace, were at school at the same time."

"Yes, I remember." Kate shot her a quick glance, putting a dry dish away in the cupboard. "I just don't remember you having much interaction with Jesse before. Mark is more your age. He worked here with your *Daed* and Grace has helped me with several big tasks around the *Haus*, but Jesse's lived away so long. We haven't seen him much till he moved back."

"Yes, he and his *Frau* lived close to one of her sisters, I believe."

"Have you seen Jesse much beyond the store? He hasn't come here to give you buggy drives or take you on walks." Her *Mamm* said, mentioning two of the things courting couples usually did.

"*Neh*, but we see each other at the store almost every day." Sarah pulled the drain plug to empty the water from the sink, turning to look at her mother. "*Mamm*, how did you—did you know you'd married the wrong *Mann* when you married my father, Jakob?"

Kate gave a deep, long sigh. "We haven't really talked about that, you and I. I want you to know I don't regret marrying your father. I wouldn't have gotten to be your *Mamm*, otherwise."

"And I will be always grateful to *Gott* for you, but you know you and Enoch have always loved one another. So, how did you know you'd married the wrong *Mann* when you married my father?"

Kate sighed, going over to sit at the kitchen table. "I don't know. There was all the business of us marrying and settling into the *Haus* your *Daed* rented. And then there was you to care for. I enjoyed that."

"And then?"

Looking at her a moment, her expression growing more serious and reflective, her *Mamm* said, "And then I got to care for the loveliest child."

"But it must have dawned on you then that you'd married the wrong *Mann*." Sarah went to sit next to her *Mamm*.

"*Neh*, not right away," Kate said. "I'm not sure we should be talking about this. It's history. Are you not…sure about marrying Jesse? He seems like a nice *Mann*."

"I'm sure my *Daed* did, too."

"If you must have it, yes. Your father was a nice *Mann*."

"Just not the *Mann* for you," Sarah commented, feeling sad and mixed up at the same time.

Sighing again, her mother finally admitted, "*Neh*, he wasn't. When I got over being mad at Enoch, I saw this."

"You and Enoch must have had a really big argument," Sarah observed, looking at her *Mamm's* youthful face. She knew about big arguments, the kind that left a hole in the chest and had her crying herself to sleep every night.

"We did." Kate looked reflective as she wiped the counter tops. "He tried to talk me out of taking a *rumspringa*, which seemed very unfair as he'd already gone on his. Actually forbid me to go on *rumspringa*."

"That probably did seem unfair." Restless, Sarah abandoned her seat at the table, pacing over to stare out the window over the sink.

Kate observed in a wry tone. "It was, but I ended up—as my *Mamm* said—cutting off my nose to spite my own face."

Giving a short laugh at this, Sarah glanced at her mom before looking back out the window. She said, "I—I don't know about marrying Jesse. There I said it! I should know! Shouldn't I? Jesse's just what I've been looking for. I should be thrilled that he asked me to be his *Frau*. He's reliable and steady. His wife and children won't have to scramble to feed themselves, if he dies."

"No." Her *Mamm's* voice was doubtful.

"And he's kind." Sarah whirled around to face her mother, as if Kate had said otherwise. "Very kind. You should have seen him with Anna after her mother was killed."

"I'm sure he's kind," Kate said, seeming bewildered that she'd suddenly found herself trying maintain an argument that Sarah was having with herself.

"He's always fair with his customers. You know, *Englischers* sometimes shop with us and Jesse is always…kind." Her sentence dwindled off.

"You aren't sure about marrying him, are you?" Kate's eyes looked both gentle and wise.

Shaking her head, Sarah said nothing for a few minutes.

Silence descended between them until she broke it, bursting out, "Why do you think Mark Fisher won't settle into a job?"

"Mark? Jesse's brother? Mark who worked here for a while?" Kate looked bewildered by the sudden change of subject.

An annoyed smile quirked the side of Sarah's mouth. "Yes, that's exactly who I mean! He worked here on the farm with Enoch—he and I worked on the cistern—but he said he doesn't see himself running a farm!"

Kate cast her a glance, asking reasonably, "Why do you care? You've agreed to marry his *Bruder*, not Mark. Jesse has a store."

"I know," Sarah said, upset with herself. "Why does it matter what Mark does?"

Her mother guessed, "Because you care for him? Are you in love with Mark?"

"He's the most foolish choice!" Sarah stalked back across the kitchen, gesturing with drama. "He's always joking and he moves from place to place, job to job. He'd make a terrible husband! And the worst of is that he could do so much better for himself. Mark's very smart! All the *Menner* he's worked for want him to continue with them! He has amazingly good ideas and he's a *gut* worker, but does he settle down! No!"

"Marrying him would be a crazy idea," her *Mamm* offered, jumping in as if trying to jump on a buggy trotting past.

"Yes! It would be!" Her cheeks felt like they'd were an even darker red.

"He's so…annoying, too." There was question in Kate's face, but she was clearly trying to be supportive.

"He is!" The passion in Sarah's voice rang out in contrast to Kate's less intense words. "And he's always, always joking and teasing. A *Mann* like him is never serious."

She stopped, memories of their terrible arguments flooding her. "Of course, he's harsh sometimes."

"*Yah?*"

Smiling faintly at her mother's valiant attempts to keep up with her vehement conversation, Sarah said in a quieter voice, "*Yah.*"

"You and he have had serious, harsh talks?"

A short laugh escaping her, Sarah said, "Yes, we have."

"About…all of this? The things about him that worry you?"

"*Yah.*"

Kate gave her a fixed stare. "These must have been…intense conversations."

"Arguments. They were arguments," Sarah corrected, her mouth twisting to one side.

"You and he have argued over these things?"

Coming to sit again at the table with her *Mamm*, she said, "Yes. We actually had—months back—a bet about it."

"You did? A bet?"

"Well, yes, he proposed a bet with me." Weaving her hands together on the table in front of her, she explained. "Mark made a few remarks about me not having married—"

"Neither has he," her *Mamm* defended.

"*Neh*, but he went on and on about me not courting with any of the *Menner* here and me just criticizing him not settling into one job. He bet me that he'd find a job to stay in before I married."

"Oh," Kate said faintly, staring at her.

"It was a stupid bet and I shouldn't have even spoken to him about his personal affairs, much less criticized him."

"You were criticizing him about his jobs?"

"I was," Sarah nodded. "It's true, but I shouldn't have said anything. Ever. He makes me so mad sometimes."

Her *Mamm* furrowed her brow and stared at her. "It takes some that way."

"What does?"

"Falling for someone," Kate responded. "Some couples are very peaceful all the time, like they never disagree. I have always suspected—knowing the reality of being married—that what's said in private is sometimes different—and some have very fiery, combative starts to their love."

"This isn't love," Sarah said emphatically, rejecting the possibility. "I refuse to be in love with Mark! I will just focus more on my goals. Yes, I-I like him, but who doesn't? He's annoying, but still likeable."

Her *Mamm's* eyebrow flew up in a silent, slightly amused response.

Ever since she'd realized the feelings burning in her chest, Sarah had resisted the reality.

"I'm not in love with him!" She absolutely couldn't marry an unstable, unreliable *Mann*. No one knew that better than she did.

"I know," Kate said, "that in your early years, your *Mamm* dying and then your *Daed's* death. All that really affected you."

"It did, of course."

"That doesn't mean," her *Mamm* reached out to cover Sarah's, "that you should marry a *Mann* you don't love, particularly if you love Mark."

"Well, I can't marry him!" Sarah said, throwing out a hand in emphasis, a hysterical note in her voice.

"You can't?"

"No! How could I do that to my *Kinder*?"

"I'm not recommending you do anything to your eventual *Kinder* or marry anyone in particular, I'm just saying it can't be right for you to marry a *Mann* you don't love. In doing so, you rob not only him of finding the right one to marry, but rob yourself, as well. *Gott* doesn't want us to have lives of sorrow and grief. You don't want to make my mistakes, do you?"

Sarah swallowed before whispering, "*Mamm*, I don't want to love Mark."

Later that evening, the light finally dying out of the sky, Sarah brushed at her tired face as she climbed the stairs to the room she shared with her younger sisters. She'd spent the entire evening with her *familye*, trying to look as if all was good with her.

The effort was exhausting for her and she still hadn't told anyone else that she was to marry Jesse. Of course, she assumed that Kate would tell Enoch, but she knew he wouldn't raise the subject with her, if she didn't bring it up. Enoch was just that way.

A shudder shook Sarah. She really didn't want to tell him. Lying to Enoch's face would be hard for her and she might stumble into talking about matters that would require lying.

If she didn't want to trouble him, although, she didn't know what that would be. Her *Daed* wouldn't ask her if she truly loved Jesse.

Quietly clicking the door closed as her sisters were asleep, Sarah didn't need a candle. She went to a small chest on her side of the room, able to move through the shadows to get ready for bed with only the dim oblongs of faint light cast through the billowing curtains that shrouded the windows.

Thank *Gott* for the breeze that made warm nights bearable.

Sneaking quietly into her bed, she turned toward the wall, hoping her sisters didn't wake to hear her sobs.

Dear Gott, I am so confused, she prayed, her tears trailing down the cheek pressed to her pillow. *I love him, Lord. I love Mark, but I can't marry him. It would be like going back, reliving that time when my own Daed died.*

Sarah reached up to quickly wipe the dampness from her cheeks. This wasn't the same, of course. Kate had a child— herself—depending on Kate for care. True, the brethren would have cared for them, but Enoch had saved Kate from marrying a *Buwe* who barely shaved.

There was no Enoch to bring her to safety and that first year of their marriage, Sarah knew was different. Kate and Enoch had worked through much. She was a kid, but most children knew when their *Eldre* were at odds.

Closing her eyes again, she envisioned herself reaching to *Gott.*

Help me know what to do, Gott? Am I being unfair to Jesse to marry him without feeling anything, but kindness for him?

And what of Mark, Lord? I love him! I love him and he makes me so angry!

As had been running through her mind, she envisioned herself married to Jesse, dutifully bearing his children, caring for Joel, Levi and Eve. Seeing Mark at *familye* gatherings and when he stopped by to help Jesse with something.

While the thought of being Jesse's wife left her with decidedly mixed feelings, the image of being his wife and seeing Mark brought a new rush of tears to her eyes.

I need your wisdom, Gott. Direct me. Help me. What shall I do?

Jesse's store was closed the next day, but Sarah left her house after breakfast anyway. A night of tears and prayer had left her convinced of what she had to do.

As the hours of darkness had crept forward—the moon rising high in the sky outside—she'd come to a reluctant, but unshakeable conviction. Now, she just needed to act on it as quickly as possible.

Marching down the dusty lane, lost in her thoughts, Sarah walked on past pastures of crops ripening in the warm summer air. As she passed, startled grasshoppers flew past as they jumped in the grass near the road, and the sun grew warmer on her shoulders as it rose. She took the turnings that led to Jesse's *Haus*, dread in her stomach as the bulk of it came into view over the horizon.

When she finally got to the *Haus*, she saw three small blonde heads bent with Anna's over a wash tub set up in the yard behind the *Haus*.

A smile tugged at the side of Sarah's mouth as she surveyed the four, laughing and giggling amongst themselves, all standing around the tub. Jesse's *Kinder* certainly saw Anna's worth.

Warming at the thought, she walked up to the back porch, without disturbing their fun.

Mounting the steps, she knocked on the door, hoping Jesse would hear her.

He must have been working in the kitchen, as he responded to her rap on the door immediately.

Seeing him through the screen door, before he pushed it open, Sarah had the thought that she must have been crazy not to fall for Jesse. He was a fine *Mann*, strong and faithful, well able to care for those in his *familye*.

He deserved better than a wife who found him only pleasant, but whose blood thundered when his *Bruder* was there.

"Jesse, can I speak with you?"

The startled expression on his face at her unexpected appearance was swiftly banished and he pushed the screen door open, saying, "Of course. Come in."

Sarah went inside, her stomach in knots. Doing this was the best choice she could make, she knew.

A pot bubbled quietly on the stove and a kitchen towel hung on a peg near the sink. The homey room smelled wonderful. The kitchen was very plain, serviceable with cabinets along one wall and an expansive, plain table near the window to the back yard.

Propping himself against the cabinets, Jesse said with a well-mannered half-smile, "Is there something in particular that brought you out this morning?"

"I need—" She broke off and started again, "Jesse, I need to say something to you."

"Okay." He seemed mystified, gesturing toward the chairs around the table. "Please, sit."

Looking toward it, she said decisively, "*Neh*, I need to stand to say this."

A shade crossed Jesse's face as he said slowly, "Alright."

She paced across the kitchen, rushing to say. "I've been up all night praying about this and I don't think you and I should marry."

He stared at her for a moment.

"You've thought better of this?"

Jesse looked startled, but, she noted, more thoughtful than heartbroken at her abrupt pronouncement.

"Why not? You have thought better of this?"

"*Neh*." She shook her head. "I'm not saying this very well."

"Tell me your reasons that we should not be married."

Mark's strong, straight, laughing image rose up in her mind's eye prompting her to take a deep breath and shove the image away.

"As I said," she repeated, "I cannot marry you."

"Why not?"

He seemed very calm and this confirmed in Sarah's head that she was doing the right thing. Relieved that he hadn't launched into a pitch to get her to change her mind, she said, "As I said, I've prayed and prayed about this."

"*Yah?*"

She went on with difficulty. "You are all the things I've wanted in a husband, Jesse. Strong and reliable. Kind and hard-working. Your *Kinder* will never go hungry or have to scramble should you be taken from this world."

He said nothing and she couldn't read his face, other than seeing his attentiveness to her words.

"You have a *gut* business and a home. Your *Frau*, Hannah, was a fortunate woman during her time on earth. You loved her and the children the two of you were raising."

"Yes," he said then, his voice quiet.

"You deserve a kind, loving home. You deserve someone who will cherish you as a husband and that your next *Frau* will think of you in this way."

He frowned, saying in a dogged tone, "I need to remarry."

"*Neh.*" She shook her head. "Not until you find the right *Maedel*. One who loves you above all others in this world."

Jesse just looked at her.

"This is not me," she acknowledged sadly. "I tried to convince myself that I could be a good wife for you, and I would have kept your *Haus*, borne your children. Made sure you had good food on the table. That I would give you what you deserve."

"I'm sure you could do all the things required," he responded, face down, his words gruff.

"I have admitted to myself and to *Gott* that, even though I've always known I want a husband like you, I'm not the woman to give you everything you deserve."

He frowned at her. "I don't believe I understand."

Sarah swallowed. This was so much harder than she'd thought.

Wiping aside a tear that had trickled down one cheek, she sniffled and forced herself to speak again. "Since I was very young, I determined that I would marry a husband with a *gut* situation, who would never leave me and his *Kinder* in dire straights. It's why I never married Able Bichsel or Timothy Musselman or any of the other *Menner* here. Oh, Able has his *Daed's* farm—"

She again fell into the argument she'd been having with herself the last few years.

"—but, he's so foolish and silly, like Moses Blatter, and Timothy is very flirty, although I'm sure his *familye* will also help him get a business."

A short bark of laughter erupted from Jesse.

"Don't you see," she said earnestly, distressed at her own perversity, "I have *gut* reasons not to marry…others…and many good reasons to marry you. Still, Jesse, I cannot."

"You can't?" He looked like his brief urge to laugh had passed, but he still didn't look heartbroken.

"*Neh.*" Sarah said the one word firmly. "It isn't the right thing to do. You deserve, as I said, to marry a woman who will love you all her days…and I just don't feel that way with you."

He stared at her, his eyes squinting a little. "Do you feel this way toward someone else?"

"My future isn't important in this," she averred. "I finally realized the question isn't whether or not I have a *Mann*, but whether I have the right *Mann*. You deserve the best woman, Jesse, and my prayers have opened my eyes to this."

For the tick of several long minutes, he just looked at her. "You're right and you deserve the best *Mann* for you, too."

Sarah realized that they were grinning at one another and that she felt as if a large stone had been lifted from her chest.

"I may never find such a *Mann*," she said, ruefully, "but that doesn't mean we should marry."

"Thank you for...for making this difficult decision. I, myself, have not felt this between us wasn't...as it should be."

"You're welcome." She smiled, reflecting that she had taken the action *Gott* wanted for her. Even if she never married—she thought fleetingly of Mark before she pushed him out of her head—she was still better off than marrying out of desperation. She'd been feeling desperate lately.

No matter how rough this path, doing the right thing felt really good.

CHAPTER TWELVE

"What's the matter, Twin?" Grace settled into the porch swing next to Mark the next morning, the chains creaking with the added load.

He glanced at her. He'd told no one of his realization that he loved Sarah. She was to marry Jesse and it was too painful to think about. He couldn't imagine spreading his anguish out for others to see. Only he thought about it all the time. The two places of respite from his tortured thoughts were his time with Grace and in the buggy shop with Daniel.

"Nothing," he answered after a few minutes, thinking that he didn't feel much peace now, not wanting to even talk to his twin about his situation with Sarah. Maybe he should spend the next several decades under a buggy at the shop. That was probably the best solution.

His twin slanted him a glance. "I know you pretty well and you don't seem yourself. So, what's bothering you?"

"I'm fine."

"No, you aren't." She pushed back to set the porch swing in gentle motion.

They cheerfully competed and hassled one other, but he could hear, this time, no challenge in her words and her expression reflected only compassionate concern.

Glancing down, Mark said half-heartedly, "I'm truly fine."

Grace patted his knee. "*Neh*, you're not."

Mark drew a deep breath. "It doesn't do any good to talk of this. What will be, will be. Some things cannot be changed."

He'd just continue, he thought, working wherever he could. He couldn't imagine loving or marrying another woman. It had taken him a long, stupid time to know his own heart, but he knew it now. Now that it was too late.

Rocking the swing as she sat next to him, Grace said nothing for several moments. "Tell me, Brother. What distresses you so?"

Her certainty made him give a short bark of laughter. "Have you not heard what I said?"

"Yes, I did, Twin," she said immediately. "I just don't believe you."

A short chuckle broke free of him and he sat swinging beside her, staring off at the distant tree line that rimmed the near pasture.

"*Bencil.*"

"I may be silly," she returned, "but I'm no more of a child than you. Tell me, Mark. What bothers you?"

"Jesse is to marry." The words fell out of his mouth, incomplete and signaling so much more than just what he said.

"Yes."

He was aware of her giving him a sideways glance.

"Jesse was married before and has talked of taking another wife," she observed. "This is to be expected."

"He's done more than talk of it." The darkness around him seemed to gather strength. "He asked Sarah to be his *Frau.*"

Grace stopped swinging. "He did, but... Didn't you speak with *Mamm* and *Daed*—with anyone—this morning?"

"I must have. We were all there at breakfast."

"*Yah,* but about Jesse."

Mystified, he shook his head. "I don't remember him being mentioned."

"Then you must have had wooly socks stuffing your head," she commented, "because *Mamm* said Jesse stopped by yesterday afternoon—he and Sarah have thought better of marrying."

"What!"

Grace drew back, her brows lifted, a comical look on her face. "Don't shout at me."

"Sorry," he said, perfunctorily. "Are you saying Sarah's not marrying Jesse? Didn't he tell our *Eldre* just last week that he was marrying her?"

His sister kept her brows raised. "*Yah*, and now he's not. He said something about them not loving one another and that they both deserve better."

"I don't understand," he said slowly.

She tilted her head to one side. "I'm not sure I do, either, but that was what he said."

Mark paused, hoping Jesse felt okay about not marrying Sarah, because this lifted a massive weight off Mark's heart.

Sarah might not be his, but he didn't have to face her across the *familye* table. At least, he told himself that he felt all better, but her not marrying Jesse still left him wishing she would marry him.

That afternoon, Anna sat with Sarah, on the Mahoning Creek bridge, their bare feet dangling in the water that eddied beneath the boards, their shoes cast aside. River birch and red maple limbs crisscrossing overhead to cast lacy shadows on the water, the two girls sat in silence as the creek water cooled their ankles.

Out beyond the trees, sunlight spangled the top of the water, the constant, soothing noise of the burbling, splashing creek filling the glade.

"Sarah?" Anna ventured, anxiety tangling in her stomach, but impelled to speak. This was her closest friend. She ached to talk with her about this.

Turning to her, Sarah said, "*Yah*?"

"Are you very sad not to marry Jesse? I mean, I know you told him that the two of you shouldn't marry, but... are you sure?" Anna stuck her foot further in the water, feeling the drag of the current.

"I'm very sure." Sarah's words echoed flat against the noise of water over rock.

Her friend certainly sounded definite and, yet Anna hesitated. "Jesse's a Godly, *gut Mann*. He's hard-working and…"

She looked down, clearing her throat. "He's kind and…and he's pleasant to look at."

"*Yah*, he's all those things. It's true." Sarah's voice held a laughing note. "Are you sure you don't want to marry him?"

Ducking her head at her friend's joking, Anna swallowed and admitted to herself that she did want to marry Jesse. She loved him.

She'd been denying her heart tugs for weeks, appalled that she felt this way about the *Mann* her friend was to marry. It was Sarah, announcing her planned marriage to Jesse, that brought reality crashing in on Anna.

She hadn't told anyone how she felt.

Anna's lip quivered as the image of herself as Jesse's *Frau* flashed through her head.

Her cheeks hot against the cooling breeze, Anna responded, "I was just pointing these things out. I thought he was the kind of *Mann* you've said you wanted."

"He's like the husband I always thought I wanted. I don't want to marry him, though."

Anna felt greatly relieved to hear the detachment in her friend's voice when she spoke of not marrying Jesse.

"Oh. Are you sure?" Sarah turned to ask Anna in a more serious tone, "Are *you* sure you don't want to marry him? You said yourself that he was a kind *Mann* and he always seems friendlier with you. More…open or something."

Anna gulped in another breath.

Since her *Mamm's* accident, and the surprise settlement to come her way, several of the *Menner* in Mannheim had come calling. None of them moved her heart or touched her reason, though. She knew it was her duty to marry again, now she even wanted to marry, after Hiram's betrayal had long pushed this option away. Anna was finally ready to marry. If only someone in this town had been the least bit interesting.

She'd found herself, however, noticing every day the *Mann* that Jesse was. Thinking of him at odd moments. Feeling happier whenever he joined in her activities with Joel, Levi and Eve.

She hadn't thought about her former husband for weeks. Hiram's abandonment had long killed whatever feelings she'd had left for him. She'd grieved his death in a bar brawl, but the stain of his actions had hung over her since he left the church and her.

With Jesse and the *Kinder*, though, her past hadn't mattered.

"I'm not saying I want to marry Jesse," Anna managed to say. "Only that he's the kind of *Mann* you've always talked of marrying."

Flushing even redder, she said, "You've often spoken of marrying a *Mann* of property, who could give his wife and children some stability. This is why you haven't married Mark."

"Mark!" Sarah yelped with sudden animation, bolting upright from the bridge side rail over which she'd been hanging. "Why do you mention him?"

"Come on," Anna chided. "You speak often of him, saying he'd not be a *gut Mann* to marry. You've said that many times. You even admitted that you like *like* him. Remember how the two of you've quarreled over his not picking a profession? You really like him, don't you? You can tell me."

Slumping back against the rail than ran across the bridge, Sarah finally said in a mournful voice, "Yes. I do like him. Like that. I'm stupid!"

The rushing sound of the water that flowed beneath the bridge filled the silence that fell between them.

"I love him," Sarah admitted in a reluctant voice.

"Oh...and you're sure," Anna ventured delicately, "that you can't marry him?"

"*Neh*," Sarah nearly sobbed. "I want to, very much, the *Schaviut*, but I-I don't see how I can ever marry him."

"You don't?"

Sarah sniffled, "Not unless I marry a *Mann* who I know may give me sorrow."

"There is much sorrow on this earth. Aren't we told to trust in *Gott* and that He's always with us? I mean, your *Mamm* wouldn't have found her way back to Enoch, if your *Daed* hadn't left the two of you in such a fix."

Her friend looked thoughtful. "*Neh*, maybe not."

"I suppose," Anna murmured, shifting her foot in the rushing water, "them finding one another could have been *Gott's* way to sort out the mess your *Mamm* and Enoch had made of things. Not that *Gott* had anything to do with your father's death, but He alone sees choices coming that we don't."

"Maybe." Sarah fell into silence, only to say a few moments later. "Jesse is too nice a *Mann* to be married to a *Frau* who doesn't love him completely. *Neh*, I will never marry, I suppose."

Sarah turned a tear-stained, laughing face toward Anna, saying with a damp hiccup, "I suppose I need to find a *Mann* I don't love and who I think doesn't deserve more than a *Maedel* who doesn't love him."

Seeing her normally-confident friend this way, Anna felt emboldened to confess, "I-I love Jesse. Now that you aren't to marry him, I can say this."

"What?!"

"I do. I-I love Jesse."

With her mouth dropped open, Sarah said nothing for a moment. Then, she exclaimed, "Why didn't I think of that?! Of course, you and Jesse make perfect sense!"

Anna ventured anxiously, "It doesn't bother you?"

"Are you kidding? No, I don't mind! I think it's wonderful. You know, I always knew you'd marry again one day."

Putting up her hand, Anna said "*Neh*! Hold on. Sarah, Jesse hasn't asked me to marry him. We have shared the raising of his *Kinder* this summer and had..." Her mind drifted into her memories. "We've had some very pleasant...moments, but we've not spoken of marriage."

How horrible if Jesse somehow overheard her even talking of this. Anna shuddered at the thought.

"But you love him?" her friend asked in a calmer tone. "This is why none of the other *Menner* in Mannheim interest you?"

Anna said with usual cynicism, "To be fair, we don't have other interesting *Menner* in Mannheim and you certainly don't want me to marry Mark."

All the laughter drained out of Sarah's face as she looked at her friend. "Do what you think best, Anna."

"No, no!" Slinging her arm over her friend's shoulder, Anna affirmed with unusual vigor, "I couldn't. I wouldn't marry Mark and he's shown no interest in me. *Neh*, You are much more important to me than is Mark."

"Maybe for you," Sarah said with irritation, "he'll settle down to be a steady, reliable *Mann*."

"I doubt that. He has no more interest in me than I do in him." After a few minutes of silence, Anna threw her friend a sideways glance. "About this mess with Mark... You've always attributed the situation with your *Daed* and *Mamm* to his not having a steady money-source, but maybe..."

Whipping around to stare at her, Sarah said, "Maybe what?"

"I know your *Daed's* situation wasn't ideal, but the state of things between him and your *Mamm* might have colored the situation for you. You were very young when he died."

Sarah kept staring at her. "What do you mean 'the state of things between' them?"

Pulling her friend to her in a brief hug, Anna said "You've said that Kate and Enoch belong together, but that means she didn't belong with your *Daed*, that they weren't happy together."

"Oh." Sarah looked away, musing, "*Neh*, when I look back on it, I can see they weren't. Not really. I was young and I don't have a complete memory of them together, but I do remember...arguments and...long periods when they didn't talk at all."

"And if they'd loved one another," Anna commented, quietly, "she'd have mourned his passing more and remembered him with nothing but love. It's one of *Gott's* gifts that the memory of loved ones who pass out of this world makes us stronger."

"This is true," Sarah said slowly.

"Maybe," Anna mused, "this is about trusting in *Gott*. He doesn't fail us, although we might not see the road. I mean, you and your *Mamm* found your way to Enoch. *Gott's* plan is to help us to the best choice, to connect us again with *Gott*. Maybe this is all about faith."

Sarah turned her head to look at Anna.

Her friend said with certainty, "*Gott* wants the best for us. Maybe it's not about gathering money for this world. Maybe He wants us to learn to rely on His good will. Money is necessary in this world, of course, but haven't you always had what you need? *Gott* has provided."

"You mean," Sarah said slowly, "that I should have faith…"

"…faith that *Gott* will lead you and Mark to wherever you're supposed to be." Anna ducked her head. "I've been trying to speak up more myself. To speak up for myself. *Gott* has given me a voice and He wants me to use it."

"Yes." Sarah waited for her to continue.

"This is what's given me the strength not to marry the foolish *Menner* in Mannheim, even though I want to be settled and to have a *familye*." Anna's smile was sweet and sad.

"Maybe…Jesse's *familye* is meant to be yours," Sarah observed.

Anna shook her head. "I would be very happy about this, but it isn't for me to speak."

"I have decided," Mark said as he and Daniel headed for the area behind the buggy shop the next day, "to accept your offer and stay on here."

Daniel stopped in midstride, grabbing his arm. "Truly? You want to work here with me long term?"

"*Yah*, if you still want." He'd spent all of the day before and much of the night wrestling with himself. "And I plan to ask Sarah to marry me. I don't know if she will, but I'm asking."

"Now that she's not marrying Jesse?"

Throwing his friend an appreciative glance, Mark said with a grin, "*Yah*, and I think I might eventually like to set up a buggy shop in Mannheim. Elizabethtown isn't that far from Mannheim, but the business here is bustling. I don't think this shop would suffer, at all."

"You're already talking of expanding to set up your own shop?" Daniel grinned at him, the two of them walking again across the area littered with buggy parts. "Sounds like you. When you settle into a place, you really settle in."

"I guess, I do."

"What has brought you to this decision?" Daniel sent him a sideways glance.

His smile fading, Mark said, "Sarah. I've always thought I'd make a choice to set up working in a job one day. She's just…pushed things along, I suppose."

"Nothing like having a *Maedel* nudge you into doing what you should be doing. That's a girl to hold on to."

"She is, if she'll have me." He wished he could feel more certain about this, but she wanted a certain kind of *Mann* and he wasn't sure it was him.

"Why would she not?"

Mark shook his head. "I've not been a 'settle down' kind of *Mann*. She was very distressed by what Kate and she went through when her dad died. Sarah may not think she can trust me to keep her safe."

"Oh, if you decide, you'll do it," Daniel said. "You are a very stubborn *Mann*."

This made him chuckle, not disagreeing. "*Yah*, I get hard-headed. I've been that way with Sarah."

"I don't know if she'll agree to marry you, but I definitely want you to work here with me. I'll even help you get set up in Mannheim, when you're ready. You're a *gut* worker, Mark. I think you'll provide a good service."

Mark stood blankly staring at the buggy frame in front of them. "I don't know how to approach her. Whether I should just drive up to her *Haus* and ask her? Or invite her on a buggy ride and ask her? Maybe I should wait a few days."

Daniel smiled faintly. "My friend, I've never seen you so uncertain."

Wheeling around to pace several steps, Mark replied, "I've never done anything like this before."

"That could be the reason. Possible rejection, though, is really scary." He jerked a stalk of switchgrass free to chew on.

Mark stopped pacing to stare at Daniel. "You think that's why I'm not sure when to speak to her?"

Pausing to scratch his chin through his beard, he said with twinkling eyes, "Probably."

Glaring at him for a minute, Mark cast his gaze upwards toward the sheltering oak branches and exhaled. "Maybe that's why I'm wavering back and forth on this. I've never before cared if others cared what I did or didn't do."

"Now, you do."

"*Neh*, no one, but Sarah. She's the only one whose thoughts truly matter."

"This is true. Her thoughts on this do matter. You're not sure that she loves you."

Mark shook his head. "I think she does, but... You know I hate saying I was wrong. I wasn't wrong to look around for the job that suits me best, but I—I think she'll only hear that I'm admitting I was not right."

"—not right and not the *Mann* she wants to marry. Rejection, my friend." Daniel leaned back against a buggy wheel attached to an axle.

Looking down at the sprigs of Virginia wild rye amid tufts of prairie dropseed that had sprung up in the back lot, Mark said with determination, "I'm sure what I want—and what I believe *Gott* thinks is best for me—but I'm not sure she'll be interested in marrying a *Mann* without an established business. After all, I'm just starting out in this."

"This is the most unnerving question to ask," Daniel quirked his mouth into that same half-smile, "but you must ask her. You must take up your faith like a coat to ask her."

"I'm just not sure how."

"You'll decide how. I have faith in you. I know Gott has faith in you and I think Sarah will, too."

"I pray so," Mark uttered in a rough, emotional voice. "I pray so."

Later that evening, Jesse crossed the yard to the barn. What he was about to do could be a really big mistake. As he approached the looming structure, he heard the lowing and snorting of the two cows that had come in to be milked. He also heard the higher notes of his *Kinder's* voices and, every now and then, one would laugh.

Jesse paused, staring sightlessly at the barn in front of him. He couldn't remember his children laughing before Anna had come into their lives.

The sun was descending, throwing pinks and golds into the dark blue sky, and the air was cooler now.

His speaking to Anna about marriage might up end his children's world again and rip another *Mamm* from them. Anna had been like a *Mamm* and they felt loved by her, he knew. Jesse just wasn't sure how she felt about him. If she said she wouldn't marry him—if she didn't love him as he loved her—the situation of her keeping his *Kinder* might become awkward.

Stepping into the dim light of the barn, a tall, star-shaped shadow cast by the beams overhead fell over him. Jesse reminded himself that *Gott* was always with him. This made him stronger and would strengthen him if she didn't love him.

The two cows were hitched to a milking post and he saw that Anna was perched there on a small stool. Joel stood next to her, patting the animal's neck. Eve balanced on her one knee while

Levi was draped over her back. Somehow, she was managing to milk the cow while in this position.

Levi's laughter rang out about something or other.

Jesse stopped again, just looking at the four of them. He loved Anna, his chest burned with it, now that his eyes had been opened. He couldn't imagine the grief of missing her. Anna not being here, not greeting him in the morning, not spending her days looking after his *Kinder* and his home.

He couldn't envision anyone else doing those things.

Drawing in a long breath, he said, "You three children. Go into the *Haus* and set the table. Anna's had some stew for supper on the stove all afternoon."

"*Yah, Daed*," Joel answered in his responsible manner.

"Anna's letting us help milk the cows!" Little Eve's high-pitched voice rang out before she started toward the barn door.

Anna smiled up at Jesse from her milking stool as Levi undraped himself from her shoulders. She called after the children, "Eve, don't you try to take that heavy pot from the stove! Let Joel help you or wait for me to come in."

Eve's thin voice could be heard faintly as she crossed the yard with her brothers. "*Yah*, Anna!"

"They are such wonderful images of *Gott*," she said, looking after them fondly. "You are a fortunate *Mann*, to have such a lovely *familye*."

He thought rashly about just asking her to join his *familye*.

Knowing he couldn't take the coward's way out, Jesse reached out his hand, drawing her to her feet, now that she was finished milking the cow.

"I want to talk to you, Anna," he said, feeling stripped bare and awkward, the feelings even larger now that they two stood alone in, but for the cows, the echoing barn.

Looking up at him as Jesse drew her to her feet, Anna tried to keep her expression from reflecting her feelings for this quiet *Mann*.

She smiled up at him unsteadily.

What she'd told Sarah was true. She loved Jesse and had, she supposed, loved him from the days when she started caring for his home and his *Kinder*.

He was a strong, loving *Daed* and a sweet, kind *Mann*. Even Sarah had said he deserved someone who loved him. Anna loved him.

Now that she knew he wasn't to marry her friend—and now that Sarah had urged Anna to pursue the relationship, she wasn't sure how to do that. She and Hiram had been together several years before deciding to marry and look where that had gone.

But she loved Jesse, more even than she'd ever cared for Hiram.

"I'm glad the children seem to be settling in here," she said. "They've met some other children at the store and even at the Sunday services."

He shuffled his feet, looking at the dirt barn floor before he looked up, taking a step closer to her. "Anna."

Jesse cleared his throat before starting again, "Anna. I'm no longer promised to any other *Maedel*...and I want to see you. May I take you for a buggy ride this Sunday after meeting?"

Anna knew her mouth had dropped open, but she couldn't help it. He wanted...wanted to see her?

"Your friend, Sarah, has—She has told me—. That is, she said..."

Startled to see Jesse this dispossessed, Anna felt compelled to interrupt. "Sarah told me that you two have decided not to marry. Is that what you're trying to say?"

"It is," he said, looking both relieved and disgusted with himself. "Are you available for a buggy ride?"

Her cheeks warm now, she knew she was blushing. "*Yah*, that would be nice."

It would be, for her, so much more than nice! Jesse wanted to see her!

"You've not promised to take a ride with anyone else?"

"*Neh*, I've not promised to take a buggy ride with anyone else." She sent him a confiding smile. "The *Menner* here seem to me to be *Buwes*, even the ones my own age that I went to school with seem young and like *Bencils*."

Flushing even more, she went on, "And I can't— I can't forget that before the settlement in my *Mamm's* accident, none of them even spoke to me after Hiram's departure and death in the bar fight."

"*Debiels*," Jesse said. "I can see why they don't interest you now. Your husband's actions weren't your fault. *Gott* has told us to forgive, even if his actions were your fault, which they weren't."

"*Denki*. That's kind of you to say."

"Anna?" He looked flushed now, saying awkwardly. "You have been good to my children. Loving...and sweet. Both kind to them and to me."

"How could I not be kind to them?" she responded, feeling as charged up and awkward as did he. "Joel and Levi are such wonderful boys and I love Eve."

Jesse looked away from her, a muscle in his cheek flexing as he stared toward the hayloft. "I love her, too, and—and I—"

He took a deep breath. "Anna, I want more from you than just a buggy ride."

Her heart now thundering in her chest, she squeaked, "You do?"

"*Yah*." He looked up at her. "I do. I want—I want to marry you. I am sure of this."

"Oh! I—I want more than a buggy ride with you, too."

Jesse stared at her, reaching out to take her hand. "You do? I mean, I'm very glad you do. I want to marry you, Anna. Even if you take me in order to keep looking after the children—and because I'm not one of the *Bencils*—I will count myself fortunate."

Looking down at her hand in his, Anna blurted out, "It's not just for the *Kinder*, and you are far from the boys with whom I went to school."

Jesse dropped her hand then, pulling her into his arms. Anna was so startled that she didn't know what to do, dropping her head on his shoulder. "Oh, Jesse!"

His hat having fallen to the barn floor, he bent his head and kissed her ruthlessly.

"Jesse!" she breathed when she could speak again.

"You are my love, Anna. You." His expression was intense as he said in a strong voice, "I want to marry you and have more children with you and spend my days with you."

"Oh, yes!" she cried, reaching up to kiss him again.

That afternoon, Sarah stared out the kitchen door at the rain pelting down in the yard between her *Eldre's Haus* and the barn, big caramel-colored puddles linked together by rivulets of rainwater. She felt peaceful inside, having given Anna her blessing to marry Jesse several days before, but that didn't mean she knew what to do about Mark.

Loving him left her jumbled up inside.

She'd prayed about it—and sent up another prayer just then—still not sure what to do. She loved Mark with her whole heart, that was no longer in question in her head. Her path would have been clearer if she didn't.

Reaching up, she wiped an errant tear from her face, glad she had the warm, cozy kitchen at her back and that her *Mamm* and *Geschwischder* couldn't see any evidence of her silent tears. She'd harassed Mark so often about his directionless path and she saw now that much of this had come from her own dilemma.

Anna was right, she saw now. She'd looked to marry Jesse or someone like him as a way to never fall into the trouble that had faced Kate. It was stupid, she saw now, but she'd forgotten that her only safety net in this world—and the best she could ever wish for—was *Gott's* love.

Sarah stepped out of the kitchen into the dim overcast light, the occasional clap of thunder overhead proceeded by flashes of lightning.

The realization of why she'd had these thoughts about her own marriage didn't remove her fears, though, but had complicated them. Having thought a lot about it and having prayed about the state of affairs many, many times, her position after her recognition that she loved Mark was no better. It was actually worse. She'd preached and preached about marrying smart to only a *Mann* who could support their family, and then fallen in love with a *Mann* who resisted doing anything she thought important.

Now that she wasn't marrying Jesse, her path to Mark should have been clear.

Sarah sighed, the sound small against the increasing thunder of the rain as it roared around her, the fresh smell of the rain mixing with a clean dirt smell and the scent of the lilac bush Kate had planted in the flower bed near nodding hydrangeas at the edge of the back porch.

Her prayers had left her knowing she had to speak with Mark about this, but she couldn't bring herself to walk smack up to him and tell him she'd been very wrong.

Just the thought had her cringing.

Maybe he wasn't interested in her.

Sarah stared into the damp gloom. Maybe she should accept that she would never marry.

"But I want to stir the pudding!" her little sister, whined inside the lit kitchen. Kate had set ablaze several lamps in the room and it glowed warm and welcoming in the cloudy, rainy dark.

A few yards away, the barn was lit, too, Enoch and the older of her young *Bruders* working inside. She'd seen the cows making their way into the barn for the evening milking and, no doubt, this was underway.

Just then, a horse and buggy drove into the yard, pulling to a stop under one of the tall trees sheltering the north side of the Haus. The buggy was so shuttered and battened against the rain that drummed against the dirt that she couldn't identify it right away.

Then, a dark-hatted figure got out to hurry and to tend to the horse. Through the driving rain she saw him. Watching this unknown, Sarah gradually recognized the *Mann* and her stomach turned upside down.

The last she'd known, Mark was working in Elizabethtown with Daniel Stoltzfus. He wasn't supposed to be in Mannheim.

She took a faltering step back from the porch railing, suddenly very flustered. Maybe she should go inside to avoid him. He must have come to see her *Daed*, although she couldn't imagine what had brought him out in the wet.

Unmoving in her shock at seeing him here, Sarah watched Mark hug his coat close to him as he jogged from the buggy to the porch. Dragging the dripping broad hat from his head after he'd reached the porch overhang, he trotted up the steps.

Sarah silently screamed at herself to go, to run inside to evade him, but she couldn't convince her feet to move.

The rain fell in sheets now all around the *Haus* and she watched in frozen longing as he jogged to the porch steps.

Slapping his wet hat against his thigh, Mark stopped when he reached the porch, squinting into the shadows there.

Holding her breath, the roar of the falling rain a steady background, Sarah realized that her soft green dress kept her from being easily seen. The thought skidded past as her gaze silently devoured him. Mark had always annoyed her and upset her, but now that she no longer denied her love for him, everything inside of her screamed with joy at the sight of him.

He took a step toward where she stood and Sarah knew she wasn't ready to calmly face him. She sent up a silent prayer for *Gott* to help her in this moment.

"Sarah?" Mark moved toward her, the shadows clearly not sheltering her. "What are you doing out here on the porch? It's raining like crazy!"

"I like rain," was all she could think to say.

Now that he stood only a few feet away, she could see the intensity in his expression, the straight line of his mouth. Looking down, he shook his hat again.

Looking down at the boards beneath her feet, Sarah prayed that he hadn't read the longing in her gaze.

"I need to talk with you, Sarah." His eyes glinted in the dim light.

"*Neh*, I should speak first." She cleared her throat.

He frowned. "You should?"

"*Yah*. This is hard to say, but I've spent a lot of time in prayer and I know I owe you an apology."

"What?" He looked startled. "Why?"

Sarah firmed her mouth and lifted her chin. "Because it wasn't my place to criticize your work choices. Ever. I was wrong and I saw that when I realized—" She stopped abruptly, appalled by what her unruly tongue had been about to reveal.

Pausing, she forced herself to muse in a reflective voice. "I was...trying to make sure I'd be safe. Trying to ensure that I'll always be alright in this world."

She shook her head, making a rueful face. "I forgot, I suppose, that this world is not my home. It doesn't matter who I marry or how stable is his work, I need to put my faith in *Gott*, not in the circumstances of this life."

"I guess it was you and Jesse not marrying brought you to this?" His flinty expression was hard to read, but he didn't look happy.

The sound of the drumming rain filled the space between them for a moment.

"It's part," she shrugged, "of why I told him we shouldn't marry."

"You told him? You decided this?"

She nodded, knowing that the dampness all around them had made the wisps of her hair that had escaped her *Kapp* to frizzle in the rainy air. "I did. I decided it. When I came to see my own motives, I knew I had to. Jesse deserves better than a wife who only married him to hide from possible bad things. *Neh*, I knew I couldn't marry him."

"I—I can't believe it."

Sarah let a half-smile ease onto her face and went on with a shrug, "I may never marry. It may not be in *Gott's* plan for me."

Mark couldn't see Sarah as an old, unmarried woman with no *Kinner* of her own.

"I sincerely doubt that," he said with a bark of laughter. "You have too many *Menner* around here interested in you."

"But I'm not interested in any of them," she said softly, wrinkling her nose.

She stood there on the porch with only a light falling from the lamps in the kitchen, her hair curling in the rain, her face ever so dear.

Mark wanted to kiss her so much in that moment that he couldn't breathe.

An evil voice whispered through his head. *Sarah had said she didn't find any of the Menner here interesting, was she thinking of another Mann in whom she might be more interested?*

Mark blinked, shaken with hatred for the imaginary *Mann*. Not able to tolerate the thought of anyone, but her in his life, he cleared his throat and hoped his silence wasn't noticeable.

"*Denki* for your apology, but—" he said before breaking off to shuffle his feet a little, "but you were right about me. I've been fighting *Gott's* plan, too."

"What? What do you mean?" Confusion was on her face.

A burst of laughter from the kitchen drew his attention.

Mark drew in a deep breath, his heart thundering in his chest, before he turned back to Sarah. *Gott* directed them to see a person's character rather than consider their appearance, but she looked beautiful: body and soul. He reminded himself that it was only human for him to notice her soft skin and crushed-berry lips, but he knew as he was standing here that he'd always regret not trying to make her his.

The way she owned up to her conceit this way showed that she had a beautiful inside, too. Her words gave him reason to hope for the first time. Maybe if she'd had all this realization about herself and had decided not to marry Jesse…maybe there was a future for them.

He supposed he'd been a cocky fool all his life, but she mattered more to him than had anything ever. Mark knew he had to speak.

"Can we—would you step over here?" He took her hand—chilly in the damp air—and moved to the end of the porch away from the block of light coming through the kitchen window. Around them the rain still thundered, shuttering the two of them from the outside world.

"Of course," she said, allowing him to tow her to the shadowed end of the porch.

The feeling coursing through him at that moment felt too intimate, too personal to share. He didn't want anyone from inside overhearing them.

Keeping her hand in his, Mark put his other hand over their clasped fingers. "I've had some realizations of my own."

"You have?" Her voice sounded breathy.

"I have." He didn't exactly know how to proceed as this was the most important conversation he'd ever had.

"I wanted to tell you that—that I've decided to take Daniel up on his offer and settle down to be his partner in the buggy shop."

She jumped a little when he said this. "Really? Oh, that's so exciting!"

"And I think we should get married. You and I." He blurted out the words.

"What!" Even in the murky light, he could see the startled confusion in her face.

"I love you," Mark said in an almost belligerent voice, "and I think we should get married."

"You do?" Sarah stared at him.

"*Yah*. I love you and I think we should live in Elizabethtown near the shop. One day I might want to open a shop in Mannheim, but we should stay near Daniel's shop for now."

"I think it's very bold of you to be making plans for the both of us!" She took a step toward him in the porch shadows, jabbing a finger in his chest. "What if I don't want to live in Elizabethtown? Maybe I want to stay here or move somewhere else!"

Mark caught her in his arms, dragging her against his chest, saying in a rough voice, "We can live wherever you want—I'll apprentice in a buggy shop wherever you want. Just tell me that you love me, Sarah, and that you'll scold me the rest of our lives."

She looked up at him from his embrace and smiled. "I do. I do love you. You make me madder than anyone else can and you make me laugh harder than anyone can."

"Marry me," he said, his words said urgently, "so you can keep me the straight and we can get mad and laugh hard together."

Yanking a hand free from his hug, she lifted it to cup his face. "Yes, I will marry you, but only with the understanding that we'll both keep the other straight."

"Can you both confess and believe that God has ordained marriage to be a union between one man and one wife, and do you also have the confidence that you are approaching marriage in accordance with the way you have been taught?"

Outside the fall sun had risen and now shone across the countryside. The air was cool and crisp and a row of buggies was lined up along the Miller *Haus* drive. Given the seriousness of this occasion, all was quiet in the stuffy house as Mark and Sarah stood before the bishop. The seats placed for wedding celebrants were filled to capacity and only the occasional child's whimper broke the silence into which the bishop spoke.

"Do you solemnly promise with one another that you will love and bear and be patient with each other and shall not separate from each other until dear God shall part you from each other through death?"

"I do," Mark responded, glancing at the woman beside him. He'd never been more certain of anything. Sarah was his heart. No matter how he'd shied away from his feelings for her, he couldn't deny that she was the partner of his days.

"I do." She glanced up at him with a smile, her expression serene and strong.

What had he ever done to deserve her? To be so fortunate as to be by her side now?

Swallowing hard, he sent up a prayer of thanks to *Gott*, praising him for the blessing of Sarah at his side. He'd been resistant to settling down to one work and one woman.

Silent while the bishop prayed, Mark looked on as the bishop took Sarah's hand and placed it in his. His heart swelling, he clasped her smaller hand in his.

Bishop Schrock then intoned, "The God of Abraham and the God of Isaac, and the God of Jacob be with you and help you together and give His blessings richly unto you, and this through Jesus Christ, Amen."

Mark again exchanged glances with his bride, her smile wide now to match his.

Around them, the quiet room suddenly became transformed with many of the women bustling off to the kitchen to help Kate bring out lunch.

Ignoring the group of friends who had flocked up to congratulate them, he pulled Sarah close, saying in a whisper only she could hear. "I promise you, wife, that I will work hard to make sure you and our children are always safe and cared for."

Sarah's gaze was misty and her smile trembled a little. "I know you will. I know you will always care for me."

"I will," he vowed. "With all the strength *Gott* gives me."

Thanks so much for purchasing Amish Prodigal! If you enjoyed this book, please consider leaving a review at   and for Amish Rogue, Book 6, the last in the Amish Vows Romance series! Authors live and die by reviews and I would be very grateful if you would do me the honor of leaving one. Thanks in advance. I so appreciate it!

.

Glossary of Amish Terms:

Aenti—Aunt
Baremlich--terrible
Bencil or Bensel—silly child
Bisskatz—skunk
Boppli—baby
Bopplin—babies
Bruder—Brother
Budder—butter
Buwe—boy
Daed—dad
Debiel—moron
Denki—Thank you
der Suh—my son
der Vedder—my father
Dochder—daughter
Dumm hund—dumb dog
Eldre—parents
Englischer—non-Amish
Fernhoodle—puzzled or perplexed
Forgeher—married couples who serve as wedding ushers
Frau—wife
Geschwischder—brothers and sisters
Goedenacht—goodnight
Goedenavond—good evening
Goedemorgen—good morning or good day
Gott—God
Grank—sick
Grossdaddi—grandfather
Grossie—big
Grossmammi—Grandmother
Gut—good

Hallo—hello
Haus—house
Hundli—Puppy
Kapp—starched white cap married females wear, black if unmarried
Keavlin—Diaper or supply bag for babies
Kinder or Kinner—children
Kinskind--grandchildren
Kleinzoon—grandson
Lappich buwe—silly boy
Liebling—sweetheart, darling, honey
Maedel—girl
Mamm—mom
Mann—man
Menner—Men
Narrish—crazy
Neh—No
Newehockers—Attendants at an Amish wedding
Nibling—one's siblings children
Onkle—uncle
Ordnung—the collection of regulations that govern Amish practices and behavior within a
     district
Rumspringa—literally "running around", used in reference to the period when Amish youth are
     given more freedom so that they can make an informed decision about being baptized into the
     Amish church.
Sauer—sour
Schmaert—smart
Schaviut—rascal
Schlang—snake
Scholar—young, school-aged person
Schweschder—sister
Schmetterling—butterfly
Verhaddelt—mixed up

Verrickt—crazy
Windle—diaper
Wunderbarr or Wunderbaar—wonderful
Yah—yes
Youngies—adolescents. Young people.

About the Author

Rose Doss is an award-winning romance author. She has written twenty-nine romance novels. Her books have won numerous awards, including a final in the prestigious Romance Writers of America Golden Heart Award. A frequent speaker at writers' groups and conferences, she has taught workshops on characterization and, creating and resolving conflict. She works full time as a therapist.

Her husband and she married when she was only nineteen and he was barely twenty-one, proving that early marriage can make it, but only if you're really lucky and persistent. They went through college and grad school together. She not only loves him still, all these years later, she still likes him—which she says is sometimes harder. They have two funny, intelligent and highly accomplished daughters and three granddaughters whose names all start with E like their great-grandmother, Eloise.

Rose loves writing and hopes you enjoy reading her work.

Amish Romances:

Amish By Choice (Amish Vows Romance, Prequel)
Amish Renegade(Amish Vows Romance, Bk 1)
Amish Princess(Amish Vows Romance, Bk 2)
Amish Heartbreaker(Amish Vows Romance, Bk 3)
Amish Spinster(Amish Vows Romance, Bk 4)
Amish Prodigal (Amish Vows Romance, Bk 5)
Amish Rogue(Amish Vows Romance, BK 6)

www.rosedoss.com
www.twitter.com - carolrose@carolrosebooks
https://www.facebook.com/carol.rose.author

Made in the USA
Las Vegas, NV
21 January 2022

41938687R00108